All I Want *for* Christmas

All I Want *for* Christmas

A Rose Gardner
Christmas Novella

Rose Gardner Investigations #7.5

Denise Grover Swank

Other Books By
Denise Grover Swank

Rose Gardner Mystery

Rose Gardner Investigations and Neely Kate Mystery

Carly Moore Mystery

Maddie Baker Mystery

Magnolia Steele Mystery

Darling Investigations

Harper Adams Mystery
Probable Cause (short story)
Little Girl Vanished
Long Gone

NOTE TO READER

This Rose Gardner novella takes place the Christmas after the end of *It All Falls Down*.

Chapter One

Rose

"You and Joe are still planning on goin' tomorrow, aren't you?" my best friend Neely Kate asked as she turned off her work computer.

A new Christmas tree farm had opened this year, and Neely Kate was dying to go. She'd never cut down a Christmas tree before, and she was sure it was going to be like all the Christmas movies she'd seen, even though we'd driven past Ned's X-mas Tree Farmpozium multiple times, and nothing about the small pine trees growing in haphazard rows screamed Christmas.

This was Neely Kate's first Christmas with her new baby, and she was determined to make it the best Christmas ever—even if Daisy was only six months old and had no idea what was going on. But the "best Christmas ever" included not only a live tree but also cutting one down, and she was sure the experience was going to be magical.

Neely Kate had brought the tree-cutting excursion up multiple times, and while my husband Joe would rather put up an artificial tree and be done with it, there was no way he'd disappoint his sister. I didn't want to disappoint her either.

I was pretty sure Ned's farm had that handled all on its own.

"It's too bad Ashley and Mikey can't come," Neely Kate said. "I think they'd really love it."

Joe and I were sharing custody of my deceased sister's kids with their currently jailed father's parents. When Violet died, she'd said she wanted me, not her husband, to raise her kids. She'd known he was involved in some shady business, but she hadn't shared the details. After Mike had been arrested, I'd gotten guardianship, but Mike's parents were fighting me on it and until Mike or the court decided, we were sharing custody. Last weekend, we'd taken the kids to Little Rock to see Santa and an ice sculpture exhibit, so Mike's parents had gotten them Thursday evening and had them until Sunday at four p.m.

"I think they are disappointed, actually, but Joe and I told them we'd wait to decorate the tree until Sunday evening when they get home."

"I hate that Mike's parents are doing this," she said with a frown. "And I know Ashley and Mikey hate it too."

She was right. They hated going to their grandparents' house. Mike's parents were of the age that believed kids should be seen and not heard. They didn't like the kids going outside to play because they got too dirty, and they didn't let them watch TV. They could play quietly with LEGO and dolls or read. I wanted the kids to have a good experience with their grandparents, so I'd tried talking to them, but my suggestions had been met with open hostility. Joe had convinced me that continuing to plead the kids' case was only hurting them, so I'd stopped. But I hated seeing them so miserable.

So, I couldn't disagree with Neely Kate. The current arrangement was disruptive to their schedule. Ashley was seven, and in our opinion, too old to be going to bed by seven, and even for three-year-old Mikey it was pushing it. Especially since our bedtime—the one Violet had followed—was eight. It threw off their sleep rhythm at our house. They'd get acclimated just to have to change it again. And since Joe and I often didn't get them home until five or later, putting them to bed at seven meant we hardly had time to do dinner, homework, and baths.

Their grandparents made them eat everything on their plate, and if they didn't, they were forced to sit at the dinner table until they finished. I was frustrated to no end. Violet would have never allowed any of this to happen, but I was powerless to stop it.

And then there was the fact that Mike's parents tended to bad-mouth us to the kids, telling them how we weren't their real guardians, we were just babysitting them until their father came home, which was highly unlikely. It only made them upset.

"I've tried convincing Mike into letting us have custody until there's a verdict in his trial, but he refuses to entertain the idea. He shuts the conversation down every time I mention it, and says his parents have a right to see *his* kids."

She made a face. "He's just bein' spiteful."

I was pretty sure she was right. I think he still blamed me for Violet's estrangement from him before her death.

"Time to change the subject," I said, feeling the familiar lump in my throat discussing the situation. "In any case, we're definitely meeting you tomorrow."

My dog Muffy, who had been sleeping in her dog bed next to my desk, popped her head up.

"Sorry, Muff," I said. "You can't go. I'm pretty sure no dogs are allowed."

Muffy put her head on her paws, looking depressed.

"Maybe next time, Muffy," Neely Kate said, leaning over to give her wiry head a rub before she stood again. "Did I tell you that Daisy and I have matching red stocking caps and mittens to go with our outfits?"

Her bedazzled hats and mittens. The glitzier the better, as far as Neely Kate was concerned. "You *do* know it's supposed to be a high of sixty-five tomorrow?"

"That's what the weatherman said, but he's wrong more often than he's right." She lifted her chin with a defiant look. "The universe knows how much I want this, and it won't disappoint me."

While Wet and Wild Walt the Weatherman was often wrong, the fact it had gotten to nearly seventy degrees today suggested that his forecast for tomorrow might be on the nose.

"Hey," she said, her face lighting up. "If Muffy could come, we could dress her up in one of those cute little costumes."

"What cute little costumes?" I wasn't sure why I asked. Neely Kate loved to put my dog in a variety of costumes, especially before she had Daisy. I was pretty sure Muffy appreciated that Neely Kate had a new subject to dress up.

"You know." She waved her hand. "The ones where their front legs are character's legs, and they have arms carrying something. Like Chucky with a knife or a pirate with a sword. I bet they have Santa ones with a beard and everything. Maybe they're even holding a bag full of toys."

Muffy looked up at me with wide eyes as though she understood what Neely Kate was saying and was pleading with me to save her.

I leaned closer to her and lowered my voice. "Don't worry, Muff. I won't let Auntie Neely Kate humiliate you like that."

"It wouldn't humiliate her," Neely Kate scoffed. "She'd look cute."

"Well, you'll have to take that one up with Joe," I suggested. "And besides, it's a moot point. I'm pretty certain Ned has a no-pets policy."

She tapped her chin. "Hmm..."

I pointed a finger at her. "I know that look. Muffy is *not* going to Ned's and she's not wearing a Santa costume." When I saw the triumphant look in her eyes, I quickly added, "Or an elf or reindeer costume." What else could she come up with? The list was endless. "Or an angel, or shepherd or drummer boy or—"

Defeat filled her eyes. "You're no fun."

"I'm loads of fun, but Muffy doesn't want to be dressed up like that." I narrowed my eyes. "She has too much self-respect."

Of course, that was the exact moment Muffy let out a loud and very stinky fart.

Neely Kate started to cough and laugh at the same time, while I waved my hand in front of my face.

"So much self-respect," Neely Kate teased. "It's really too bad she's not comin'. Did you know that Ned has a professional photographer on site to take photos? Muffy could get her picture taken on Santa's lap. I think I've convinced Jed to wear the red scarf that matches ours." Her bottom lip stuck out. "Can you believe he's refusin' to wear the matchin' hat?"

Part of me was surprised that Jed had refused. He practically gave Neely Kate anything she wanted, but I'd also seen the hat, so I was with him on that decision. Jed was a confident man, and his masculinity was rarely threatened, but I was sure that the words "Ho, Ho, Snow" written with silver sequins was close to the line.

"Maybe he could just wear a red flannel shirt," I suggested. "You know, to go with cutting down a tree. He'll look like a lumberjack."

Her eyes sparkled with excitement. "That's a great idea! I need to find one before I head home." She grabbed her bag. "What are you and Joe up to tonight?"

I laughed. "Nothing. We have a date night with a pizza and our TV. And after Hope goes to bed…" My eyebrows lifted with innuendo.

A grin spread across her face. "You gonna leave soon to pick up Hope from daycare?"

I shook my head. "Joe texted that he and Bruce Wayne finished their job early. He was headed to the daycare and asked me to pick up the pizza."

She paused at the door, a faraway look. "I never in my wildest dreams thought I'd be this happy. I have everything I ever wanted." She shook her head. "How is that even possible?"

"Because you're a good person, who deserves good things," I said. "Call it divine intervention, God's will, or karma, but Jed and Daisy are just as lucky to have you as you are them." I made a shooing motion. "Now, go enjoy your night. We'll meet you at the Christmas tree lot at three."

"Have a good night, Rose," she called as she walked out the door, looking over her shoulder at my dog. "You too, Muffy."

Muffy lifted her head and let out a bark in response.

Neely Kate had replaced our single bell attached to the door handle with a red velvet ribbon covered with multiple bells, so it jangled merrily as the door closed behind her. She'd decorated the rest of the office too. White lights were strung at the tops of the walls, and a small artificial tree stood in front of one of the windows. She'd even hung small stockings along the window ledge for all the employees with their names written in gold glitter. The place felt even cozier than usual.

I studied the design on my computer screen, considering calling it a night myself. This was usually our slowest time of year, but we'd had an uptick of people getting a jump start on their landscaping for the upcoming year. I suspected the warm weather had something to do with it. But all the requests meant I had lots of designs to work on, and I'd learned that when I told myself I could work at home, I rarely got any work done. I was too busy being with my family.

I texted Joe that I was going to stay another half hour then order the pizza and pick it up on the way home.

We're just hanging out. See you when you get home.

Then he sent a selfie of him with Hope on his lap, gnawing on a teething toy, not that I was surprised. She'd had a tooth coming in for nearly a week and had been chewing on everything in sight. Joe was grinning and she was snuggled against him. All I wanted was to be with them, so I ordered the pizza, shut off my computer, and headed out. Maybe I could get some work done this weekend.

Chapter Two

Neely Kate

I knew Rose thought I was going overboard with Christmas, and I couldn't say I blamed her. I mean, I was making such a big deal out of going to Ned's X-mas Tree Farmpozium when even I knew the place was a disaster. But I'd never had much of a Christmas as a kid. For the first twelve years, it had just been me and my mother, and whichever loser boyfriend was her flavor of the month. Most years, we never even had a Christmas tree, not unless her boyfriend wanted one. We didn't have any stored decorations, so if we got a tree, we'd make paper snowflakes, glitter-covered construction paper ornaments, and string popcorn garlands, although my mother would quickly grow tired of doing any of the crafting and left it up to me. (I supposed those Christmas ornaments helped form my love for bedazzling. The shinier the better.)

There were no stockings hung by the chimney with care—not that the places we lived ever had chimneys. There were definitely no presents.

The exception was the year I'd turned ten. My mother had somehow managed to pick herself a nicer boyfriend. When he realized my mother hadn't planned to give me a Christmas, he'd brought over a real tree that somehow looked even worse than the one on the Charlie Brown Christmas special. He'd even bought a few decorations. The topper was when he came home on Christmas Eve with two presents—one for my mother and one of me. On Christmas morning, there was an extra present under the tree for me that said it was from Santa.

O Come, All Ye Faithful was playing as I opened it—a baby doll who pottied on the provided plastic toilet. I was ten going on twenty at that point, and I thought I was too old for dolls, let alone dolls that peed, but it didn't stop my tears of gratitude. I gave him the biggest hug, and kissed his cheek, and he told me Santa had noticed I was a good girl. I knew it was from him, but I played along, catching the dark look in my mother's eyes.

She broke up with him two days later.

It was no secret why. She'd claimed she was protecting me because he was a pervert for giving me a gift like that, but we both knew it was because he'd given me more attention than she ever had. Jenny Lynn Rivers was an attention whore who always wanted the spotlight on herself, and she saw me as competition.

Less than two years later, she dropped me off at my grandmother's farm and she never looked back.

Christmas at Granny's was different than with my mother. There was always a tree and plenty of stockings and lots of food —a luxury that had often been in short supply with Jenny Lynn. But there were also lots of people and lots of noise and lots of confusion. Sometimes, I felt lost in the crowd.

My cousin Witt was closest to me in age, and we were friends when we were younger, but he was a rowdy boy who was rough and tumble with our older cousins. Christmases with the Riverses were better, but I still didn't feel like they were mine.

So, this Christmas, I'd decided it was going to be the Christmas I'd always dreamed of as a child. I swore that Daisy would have everything I hadn't—trees with store-bought orna-ments, cookies, carols, and lots and lots of presents.

Which meant I was going overboard on everything.

So, I knew Rose thought I was being ridiculous even if she was too kind to say so. I suspected Jed secretly did too. Sure, Ned's X-mas Tree Farmpozium was bound to be lame, but cutting down a Christmas tree had always been one of my dream Christmas activities, and once Jed found out, he swore he'd make it happen.

But he still refused to wear the bedazzled hat I'd made him.

There was only so much a man could do for the woman he loved before he had to draw the line.

I had to admit that Rose's idea for the shirt had been a brainstorm, and I wasn't sure why I hadn't thought of it. Maybe it was because I'd been too busy bedazzling everything that didn't move.

Nicholson's Farm Supply was on the way home, so I pulled into the parking lot then headed straight for the flannel shirts in the men's section. I was shuffling through the rack when I heard a familiar voice behind me.

"Well, well, well. I'm surprised to see you here, Neely Kate Colson."

I spun around and propped a hand on my hip, giving Carter Hale a good-natured glare. "It's Neely Kate Carlisle now, and before that it was Neely Kate Rivers. You, of all people, should know I hate that name." He'd been my divorce attorney, after all.

"My apologies," he said, making a slight bow.

I narrowed my eyes. "What on earth are you doin' slumming at a farm store, Carter Hale?"

He shrugged as a cheesy grin lit up his face. "Maybe I'm finding a flannel shirt, same as you."

"Doubtful." I shook my head. "I struggle to see you in a flannel shirt…although *maybe* a flannel tie."

He let out a deep laugh. "I'll have you know I've worn flannel shirts in my day."

"When did *you* ever wear a flannel shirt?"

"I wore plenty of them when I was a boy. My mother used to shop here regularly."

That caught me by surprise me, although I wasn't sure why. I'd heard that Carter was raised in these parts. In fact, I was pretty sure his family lived close to the Louisiana border, and most people down that way didn't have money. I supposed I'd imagined Carter being born in his suit and tie.

"Maybe so, but that doesn't explain what you're doin' here now."

He shrugged. "Maybe I'm looking for a Christmas present. It 'tis the season, after all."

I gave him a saucy grin. "You're tellin' me you have someone who you actually buy Christmas presents for? Your receptionists don't stick around long enough to warrant a Christmas gift." I tilted my head. "Can Skeeter Malcolm wear flannel shirts in the federal prison?" I motioned up and down my body. "I thought he was strictly wearin' orange jumpsuits."

A serious look crossed his face, and he quickly tried to cover it with a smile that didn't reach his eyes. "I still have family in these parts." He studied my face for a long second, then surprised me when he asked, "Are you happy with Jed?"

My mouth parted in shock. "Why would you ask me that?"

He looked grim as he turned to the clothes rack and started sorting through shirts, moving the hangers one by one. "Just checking on my favorite client," he said. "Giving you part of the whole customer care experience."

I knew it was more than that. Carter had been interested in me at one point, but I couldn't help thinking that this had something to do with his loyalty to his boss. Was this because Jed left Skeeter? Was Skeeter out for revenge because he'd been arrested and Jed had gotten off scot-free?

But Carter had gone above and beyond to help me find my wayward husband, Ronnie, even if his attempts hadn't been unfruitful. I decided to give him the benefit of the doubt. "I'm good. I'm happy," I said softly. "I love my life with Jed and our baby."

He nodded slightly as he continued to look at the rack, shuffling the hangers, metal screeching on metal. "I was going to call you," he said, still keeping his gaze on the hangers. "I feel like I should warn you…the FBI will be contacting Jed after the first of the year."

I felt like I was going to pass out. Suddenly, every dream I had of my life with Jed felt like it had been tossed onto a funeral pyre and Carter was holding the torch. "What?" I asked breathlessly. "Why?"

He glanced at me. "The *real* question is, why haven't they already? Haven't either of you wondered? Jed Carlisle was a known associate of James Malcolm for over a decade. Seems to me they'd think Jed had plenty of dirt to bury Skeeter."

I shook my head. Sure, we'd worried that they'd question him, mostly because Jed's hands weren't clean. He'd done things, some of which he wasn't particularly proud of, and there was no statute of limitations on some of them. But Skeeter had been arrested last June, and after so many months, we thought we were in the clear.

"Are you sure?" I asked, my voice shaky.

He turned around to face me. "About ninety-five percent sure."

I drew in a sharp breath. "Are they gonna try to pin something on him?"

He hesitated. "Jed should get an attorney."

My head started to become fuzzy. "I thought *you* were his attorney."

"I'm *Skeeter Malcolm's* attorney. If Jed uses me, it will look guilty by association, and even if he was complicit in this mess, he still couldn't use me. It would be a conflict of interest."

"How is it a conflict of interest?" I asked in dismay.

He leveled his gaze and said firmly, "He needs to get an attorney, Neely Kate."

I backed up a few paces, and Carter followed, gripping my elbow. "Do you need to sit down? You look like you're about to pass out."

I didn't respond, but he gently guided me to the boot section a few feet away and helped me sit on a bench.

I took several breaths to calm down, but my panic continued to rise. "What are the chances they're gonna charge him with something?"

Carter squatted in front of me, compassion filling his eyes. "I suspect they're gonna want dirt on Skeeter. They might threaten him with charges, then offer him some kind of immunity deal to get it. Which means he's gonna need a shark of a lawyer. I'd ask Deveraux for some suggestions."

My eyes flew wide. "Mason?"

He nodded.

"But Mason's not even around here anymore. Last I heard, he got a job with the secretary of state up in Little Rock, not to mention he's on the prosecuting side of the law."

"Neely Kate, this'll be happenin' up in Little Rock. Mason may not be Jed's friend, but he's *your* friend. He'll help you."

I tried unsuccessfully to swallow the lump of fear in my throat. "Just like you're helpin' me now."

He nodded. "I tried contacting Jed, but I think he's blocked my number."

"That was stupid," I grunted.

Carter laughed. "I always liked you, Neely Kate. You never held back any punches." He paused, then said, "Skeeter liked you too."

I made a face, then after a second said, "My feelings for that man are complicated."

"That's fair."

I gave him a sad smile. "Isn't this where you threaten me that Jed shouldn't rat Skeeter out…or else?"

He slowly shook his head. "No. I'd never do that to you, Neely Kate. You deserve every bit of happiness that you can get. I hate telling you this, especially so close to Christmas, but I didn't want you to be caught unaware. Jed needs to find a lawyer fast and come up with a game plan."

Tears filled my eyes, and I reached out and put my hand on his shoulder. "You're a good friend, Carter. Thank you."

"Shhh!" he said, glancing around. "Don't go ruinin' my badass reputation."

I laughed, just like he expected me to, but he'd said what he had to say and gave me what comfort he could. The rest was up to me and Jed now.

I stood and he stood with me. "Thank you," I said, my voice breaking.

"Ah, Neely Kate." He tapped the underside of my chin. "Chin up. Get a badass attorney nearly as good as me, and you'll both be okay."

"You sayin' I shouldn't find one better or equal to you?" I teased, surprised I had it in me given the news I'd just heard.

"There's no one equal to me, let alone better," he scoffed.

"Humility was always a good look on you, Carter."

"I just call it as I see it." He walked over to the rack and grabbed a red flannel shirt with black plaid stripes, then handed it to me. "Here, this'll be tight on Jed's arms, but you'll appreciate the view."

"Who said I was lookin' for a shirt for Jed?"

He grinned. "Who else would you be buyin' a men's shirt for?" I started to tell him I could have been buying a Christmas gift for my brother, but he'd already turned and headed for the exit. I hadn't even had a chance to thank him. Which, I suspected, was how he preferred it.

It wasn't lost on me that he hadn't bought anything. And it

also wasn't lost on me that he'd likely followed me here, so we'd be alone when he shared his dreadful news.

Now I had to go home and tell Jed.

No, not yet.

I didn't want to spoil the weekend. Carter said the Feds would be calling after the first of the year, which meant I had time to tell him later.

Chapter Three

Rose

Joe was in the living room with Hope on his lap when Muffy and I walked in through the front door, and Joe's face lit up when he saw me. Muffy made a beeline for the sofa and jumped up, taking turns covering first Joe's then Hope's faces in kisses. Hope burst into giggles and put her arm around Muffy's neck.

"We missed you too, Muffy," Joe said, then rubbed her ear for several seconds before he stood, holding Hope's back to his front, his arm around her chest and tucked under her armpit. He closed the distance and leaned in to give me a quick kiss.

"Want to trade?" he asked, reaching for the pizza box.

I let him take the pizza and scooped Hope into my arms. She smiled at me and babbled as her hand patted my face.

"There's my sweet baby." I kissed her forehead and held her close. My heart swelled when she leaned into me and patted my chest.

Joe gave Muffy one more head rub before he headed into the kitchen.

I followed, and Muffy jumped off the sofa and trotted behind me.

"Has Hope eaten yet?"

"Nope," he said. "We were waiting for you. I knew you'd probably want to feed her."

As he put the pizza box on the table, I noticed a jar of baby food carrots and a small spoon on the highchair tray. A couple of plates were already on the table along with a small stack of napkins.

I gave Hope another kiss, then set her in her highchair and put her bib over her clothes. I twisted the lid off the baby food jar as Joe opened the box and put a slice of pizza on a plate, then set it in front of me.

Muffy settled into her dog bed underneath the window looking over the barn and field behind the house.

The house felt quiet and unsettling without Ashley and Mikey there, but I stuffed the thought down and focused on my baby.

I gave Hope a spoonful of carrots, some of which got smeared on her lips. "How did the Ferrimen job go?" Since most people didn't need landscaping done in November and December, Bruce Wayne had come up with the idea to install Christmas lights, and since Joe was working for Bruce Wayne, he installed them too.

"Pretty good," he said, grabbing his own slice. "We got two more jobs out of it."

I shot him a quick glance. "That's awesome." I wasn't surprised. Most of the work they'd done had come from referrals or people noticing the signs they put out in the yards of the houses they'd installed. It was two weeks before Christmas, but they had more jobs than they'd had two weeks before. "Installing Christmas lights was a great idea."

"Bruce Wayne gets all the credit," he said before he took a bite of his pizza.

"True, but you got the deal on Christmas lights."

"Speaking of," he said before he swallowed. "We're gonna need more lights, which means I need to head down to Shreveport bright and early on Monday."

I nodded in acknowledgment. "Do you think you'll get the same deal?"

"I'm gonna try."

I cast another glance over my shoulder. "How are you doin' with all of this?" I asked quietly.

His brow lifted in confusion. "Drivin' to Shreveport?"

"No, workin' for Bruce Wayne." I made a face then turned back to Hope, whose mouth was open, waiting for her next spoonful of carrots. "Workin' for me."

"Rose," he said tenderly, "we've discussed this. I'm good with it. It's fine."

He'd quit his job as the chief deputy sheriff last spring when I'd faced down Denny Carmichael, a county drug czar, as well as the international cartel, Hardshaw Group, so he could protect me. I was dealing with criminals, and his duty as a sheriff deputy obligated him to report what he encountered. By quitting, he freed his conscience, but I'd worried he'd regret it in the long run. While Joe was good at landscaping, I was pretty sure he didn't love it. Still, he liked working on home repair and remodeling projects, and he was considering buying a home to flip after Christmas.

I bit my bottom lip. "If you change your mind…"

"Maybe I will in the future, but for now, I'm enjoying havin' more time with you and the kids. I would have never been able to pick Hope up from daycare at three o'clock if I still had my old job." He winked. "And I wouldn't have had time for the incredibly hard job of setting out the plates for pizza."

I laughed as I shook my head. "Very true."

"Change of subject." He leaned forward and made a face at Hope. A huge grin spread across her face. "Are we still on to go to the Christmas tree farm tomorrow?"

"Of course. Neely Kate's gotten her and Daisy and Jed matching outfits to have their photo taken in and everything."

He chuckled. "And Jed's goin' along with this?"

"You know that man would walk on water if Neely Kate asked him to."

"True, but I'm struggling to picture him in an ugly sweater."

"I'm pretty sure she was picking up a red flannel shirt for him on the way home today, so prepare to be disappointed."

"There's always Christmas," he said. "Maybe he'll wear one then."

I laughed, which made Hope giggle.

"What's so funny, little miss?" I asked as I scooped carrots off her face then put the spoon in her mouth.

"Are we dressin' up tomorrow?" Joe asked, and I heard the hesitation in his voice.

I glanced back at him. "Scared I'm gonna make *you* wear an ugly sweater?"

"Sort of," he admitted.

I laughed again. "No worries. I don't plan on makin' a big deal of this excursion. I mean, we've both seen the tree lot. If I had my way, I'd already have a tree up while the kids were here to help decorate, but this was so important to Neely Kate, so…"

"You're a good friend and sister-in-law."

"She's done a heck of a lot more for me than go to a Christmas tree farm. Besides, maybe it'll be fun. I just wish Ashley and Mikey could come." I hesitated. "Maybe I should try again to see if Mike's parents will let us pick up the kids for a couple hours to go to the tree farm."

"I already tried, Rose," he said quietly. "Mike's dad hung up on me."

My heart sunk. "Why do they have to be so nasty? They're just hurtin' the kids."

"I think they're scared Mike's gonna go to prison and the judge is gonna give them to us."

"Holdin' onto them like this isn't gonna help their case."

"You and I both know that. Too bad their attorney isn't tryin' to drive that point home." Our attorney had told us that the more amenable we were, the better our chances would be to get full custody. She said the judge we'd been assigned placed a lot of weight on flexibility and accountability.

"At least we have them for Christmas Eve and Christmas morning," Joe said. "You know they'll love havin' everyone here for Christmas Eve dinner."

Bruce Wayne and Anna didn't have any family, and Maeve was planning to drive up to her son's house in Little Rock on Christmas Day. Jonah Pruitt, my friend and the pastor of the New Living Hope Revival Church, and his girlfriend were coming over after we all attended Christmas Eve service. Neely Kate and Jed had been invited to a big gathering at her granny's, but when Jed had heard one of her aunts was bringing roasted raccoons for the main course, he suggested they skip the family dinner, eat with us, then go over later.

"They *are* excited about it." I hesitated. "Are you still okay with hostin' this dinner? We can always cancel if it's too much." It was a lot of people, and it suddenly occurred to me that maybe he'd just agreed to it because I'd been so excited about it. He was a lot like Jed in giving me pretty much anything I wanted, and I tried my best not to take advantage of it. Still, sometimes I wasn't entirely sure he was as happy about my plans as I was.

"I'm lookin' forward to it too, Rose," he assured me. "We'll have Christmas morning with the kids until Mike's parents pick them up at noon, and then we'll go over to Jed and Neely Kate's for dinner." He winked. "*Although* I was thinkin' about tryin' to score an invite to Granny Rivers's Christmas Eve dinner. I've never had roasted raccoon before."

"If you're lucky, they might have leftovers, and Jed can bring you some."

He licked his top lip. "Lucky me." Only the way he was looking at me made me think he wasn't thinking of roasted raccoon. "What do you say after Hope goes to bed, we Netflix and chill? If we're gonna be kid-free, we might as well take advantage of it."

I laughed. "I suspect that doesn't mean what you think it does."

His eyes danced with mischief. "I know exactly what it means."

Chapter Four

Rose

Neely Kate and Jed were already at Ned's X-mas Tree Farmpozium when we pulled into the lot, not that I was surprised. I suspected they had arrived at least fifteen minutes early due to Neely Kate's excitement. They were pointing out an animatronic reindeer to Daisy who was in Jed's arms.

"That reindeer's new," Joe said. "A whole lot of this stuff is new."

I hadn't seen the tree farm in a few weeks, but Joe was right. Ned had put a lot more effort into making it more Christmasy. There had been a portable shed on the property, but now there was a food cart off to the side with a few people standing in line in front of it. Christmas lights had been strung from tall poles, giving the place a cozy vibe, and multiple inflatable Santas, reindeer, and elves were scattered around the lot, along with multiple animatronics. A tractor with an attached wagon was pulling up to the shed. Several people were sitting on hay bales in the back of the wagon and when it came to a stop, a guy pulled a Christmas tree out of the back.

"I know most of this stuff wasn't here a couple of weeks ago,"

I said. "One of my clients told me how boring this place was, not that it dissuaded Neely Kate."

"Maybe Ned had a lot of people sayin' that, so he spruced up the place," Joe said as he pulled into a parking space, then he shot me a cheesy grin. "Get it? Christmas tree lot. Spruce?"

I groaned good-naturedly. "Don't you think you're too young for dad jokes?"

He laughed. "I *am* a dad, though." His gaze softened as he glanced in the backseat in the direction of Hope's car seat. "Sometimes I can't believe this is my life. You and Hope …" His voice tightened as his eyes turned shiny. "A year ago, I never thought this was possible."

I reached over and snagged his hand. "I love you, Joe. I wouldn't have it any other way." But even as I said the words, part of me felt like a traitor. Joe wasn't Hope's biological father—that man was sitting in a federal prison in eastern Arkansas waiting for his trial. He'd given up a plea deal to save me and Hope last spring, and some days my guilt was overwhelming.

Joe studied my face, recognizing what I was thinking. "Skeeter Malcolm wanted that, Rose. He chose it for you and Hope."

Tears filled my eyes. "But—"

"No but," he said gently. "Besides, he's guilty of everything he's been charged with, and you know it."

He was right, but it still didn't feel right. I swiped a tear from my cheek.

"I always thought he was a selfish bastard," Joe said, but there was no malice in his voice, "especially how he treated you after you told him you were pregnant, but then he proved he really does care about the both of you." The corners of his lips lifted in a sad smile. "He gave up his life for yours and Hope's, and while I still don't like the asshole, I respect the hell out of him for it."

Joe had only seen the bad parts of James, but James had shown me that, deep down, he was a man trapped by his circumstances. I'd brought out the softer side of him, the part he hadn't known he was capable of, and I couldn't help feeling guilty about that too. The man I met several years ago wouldn't have given up his freedom for anyone, possibly not even Jed, his previous right-hand man and ex-best friend. Yet, he'd done it for me and a baby he'd claimed he wanted no part of. "I can't help thinking if I hadn't gotten involved with him, he wouldn't be where he is now."

"By your own admission, he was an asshole when you met him. The way I see it, he redeemed his soul. He would have never done that without your influence."

I didn't respond, because while I suspected he was right, I was still racked with guilt.

"Hey," Joe said, stroking the back of my hand. "I didn't mean to dredge this up. I was just feeling overwhelmed with gratitude." Leaning closer, he pressed a gentle kiss on my lips. "I'm a very happy man, Rose."

A wry smile twisted my lips. "At Ned's X-mas Tree Farmpozium? That's a very sad statement, Joe Simmons. It's a far cry from the Simmons family's fancy Christmases."

He made a face. "Don't remind me. And besides, there's no Simmons money left after the FBI took it all, not that I wanted a penny. I was glad to be done with it." After his father's death nearly two years ago, the FBI had raided the Simmonses' house in El Dorado and his mother had been tossed out penniless. Joe had told her he was done with her and their messed-up family, and she'd moved in with her elderly parents who weren't people of means.

A loud bang hit the passenger window next to me. I jerked in surprise and turned around to see Neely Kate rapping on the window.

"You all can make goo-goo eyes at each other when you get home," she said through the glass. "We're burnin' daylight."

I gave Joe a grin. "Let's make this the best Christmas tree cutting excursion ever."

"As long as it doesn't resemble the scene from Chevy Chase's *Christmas Vacation*, I'm good."

We got out and Joe leaned into the backseat to unstrap Hope from her car seat.

"What were y'all talkin' about?" Neely Kate asked, bouncing Daisy on her hip. Daisy was wearing a red and black flannel dress with black tights, and a red and black hat on her head, covering her wispy blond hair. The collar of the dress and the brim of the hat were bedazzled with silver gems. Neely Kate's outfit matched Daisy's. I would have looked ridiculous if I'd worn it, but Neely Kate pulled it off beautifully. She and Daisy looked like they belonged in a Hallmark movie.

Before I could answer, she looked me up and down and made a face of disapproval. "Is that what you're wearin'?"

I glanced down at my lightweight Christmas sweater and jeans. "I didn't know there was a dress code."

"We're gonna get pictures."

"We can take pictures, Neely Kate," Joe said as he lifted Hope out of the car. "We followed the theme and wore Christmas clothes." He pointed to his long-sleeved black T-shirt that had a Santa leaning back and laughing while holding his hand against his belly. Minions dressed as elves surrounded him.

Neely Kate sent him a scowl. "That's a T-shirt with *Minions*."

Joe shrugged. "Hope likes it." His gaze dropped to her face. "Don't you, baby girl?"

She babbled in response and waved her pudgy fists.

"Your family is the one getting photos, Neely Kate," I reminded her. "Not us."

"You don't want a family photo?" she asked with a frown.

"We had professional photos taken before Thanksgiving to send out with our Christmas cards." Mike's parents had been furious when they found out we'd included Ashley and Mikey in the photo session, then they were even more furious when they realized we'd sent them out in our cards. I'd considered just sending a photo of me, Joe, and Hope, but they were part of our family, whether Mike's parents liked it or not. Besides, Ashley had been so excited about signing her name in the cards, there was no way I was telling her she wasn't included.

"You can't have too many Christmas photos," Neely Kate protested. "Besides, I thought we could all get photos together."

"We'll take photos with you if you want. We'll make y'all look good."

Joe laughed as Jed walked up, carrying a band saw and an ax. He was wearing jeans and a red and black flannel shirt. The sleeves were rolled up to expose his forearms. "Ned says the biggest trees are out on the far south side."

"How tall are we talkin'?" Joe asked as he opened the tailgate with one hand while holding Hope on his hip. "Seems like those trees can't be more than five feet."

"I want a big one," Neely Kate said. "I want it to touch the ceiling."

Jed laughed. "I know. You've told me about ten times today."

"If you want a seven-foot tree," Joe said, "I think you came to the wrong place."

I walked around and took the baby from Joe so he could get the stroller out of the back.

"Don't worry," Jed said. "Maybe we can put it on a box,"

Neely Kate glanced around the parking lot. "I wish there was snow."

"Not to worry," Jed said with a wink. "Ned's got a backdrop with snowy mountains, and a hay bale covered in cotton to look like a snowbank. He's even got a plastic snowman and reindeer."

Neely Kate frowned. Jed walked over to her and pulled her into a sideways hug.

"I just want it to be perfect," she said wistfully.

"It will be," Jed assured her. "As long as it's us three, it could smell like dog shit out here and it would still be perfect."

She smiled up at him.

"Unlike Jed," Joe said in a teasing tone, "I won't call it perfect if it smells like dog shit, but you can make it up to me later." He set the stroller on the ground and popped it open before he closed the tailgate. "You ready to go find the tallest tree on the farm?"

"Jed's right," Neely Kate said. "No matter what happens, it's gonna be perfect."

I wasn't sure about perfect, but I suspected it would be entertaining.

I put Hope in the stroller, strapped her in, then handed her a teething toy.

We headed through the parking lot toward the farm. Several families were walking out into the rows of pine trees, and Neely Kate was antsy to get out to the perfect tree. She got irritated when Joe and Jed stood at the edge of the lot, discussing their plan of action.

"All the good trees are gonna be gone," Neely Kate said, shifting Daisy to her other hip.

Jed handed Joe the ax and saw, then took his daughter. "Okay, fine. We've got a plan. Let's head out."

The guys took the lead, leaving me pushing the stroller and Neely Kate to follow.

"Joe," I called out to them, "don't you need to get an ax or a saw?"

"We're only gonna cut one tree down at a time," he said, glancing over his shoulder.

"You could have a tree cutting competition," Neely Kate said. "See who chops their tree down the fastest."

That sounded like an ER trip in the making. "Maybe let's not."

We trudged up a small hill meandering through the crooked rows, and I couldn't help thinking how the trees should have been planted and how I would have done it differently.

After about five minutes, we reached the back part of the lot and reached a section of barely five-foot trees. This section had several families picking out trees, and there were several spots where trees had already been cut down.

"I knew we should have come last weekend," Neely Kate groaned. "All the good trees are gone!" She shot me an accusatory look.

"I'm sorry," I said, lifting a hand in surrender. "But we promised the kids we'd take them to Little Rock."

She made a face. "Yeah, you're right. Sorry."

I gave my friend a worried glance. I knew she was all keyed up about having the best Christmas ever, but she seemed anxious about it, like finding the perfect tree was a life and death matter.

"You okay?" I asked her in a worried tone.

Her eyes widened. "Why wouldn't I be okay?"

"Well … you just seem …" I hesitated, looking for the right words. "On edge."

Her head dropped and she studied the ground as we walked. "I'm fine."

"You don't seem fine."

She lifted her face and offered me a smile that looked as fake as a three-dollar bill. "I'm just hangry, is all. I didn't eat much for lunch."

I'd seen firsthand how surly she could get when she skipped a meal, but this seemed deeper than that. Like her soul was heavy. Was all this perfect Christmas stuff making her think about her mother? "You know," I said carefully, "Christmas is about the people you're with, and no matter how big or short your tree is, you'll have Jed and Daisy." I grimaced. "Sorry. I didn't mean for that to sound so preachy."

"No, you're right," she said, her voice breaking. She darted a glance to Jed and Joe who were about ten feet in front of us, then turned back to me. "I can't talk about it here."

Now I was really worried. She obviously didn't want the guys to hear her, and I was pretty sure she didn't keep secrets from Jed. "You'll tell me later?"

"Yeah. Sure." She picked up her pace and caught up to Jed, grabbing his free hand in hers.

Joe glanced over his shoulder at me. "You doin okay back there?"

"We're good."

But he slowed down until we reached him then started talking to Hope, telling her he'd try to make sure we didn't bring home a tree with a live squirrel.

"Mikey would like it if you did," I said with a grin. *Alvin and the Chipmunks* is one of his favorite movies."

He grinned. "I was keeping with the *Christmas Vacation* theme. I'm sure a squirrel in the tree would top his grandparents' sad ceramic Christmas tree that they stick on a table in their living room window, but I think I'll make sure the wildlife sticks to their natural habitat."

"I'm all for leaving the wildlife behind."

When we reached the end of the farm, Neely Kate walked around the trees in that section three times, before she finally picked out what she called the "nearly perfect" tree. While it was full, it was barely five feet tall.

"Jed's right about the box for a stand," Joe said. "I can build you one when I get home. I have some spare lumber out in the garage."

Neely Kate sighed. "It still won't be tall enough."

"What about a tall tree topper?" I suggested. "Maeve ordered some in for the nursery gift shop. There's one that's over a foot tall and it's pretty too."

"There you go," Jed said. "Problem solved."

It obviously wasn't what she'd wanted, but she seemed to accept Plan B, then moved on to the tree-cutting part of the expedition. "Do I get to watch you chop down a tree now?"

Jed laughed. "You know it." He handed Daisy over to her and winked as he took the ax from Joe, flexing his muscles. The veins on his forearms stood out.

I pretended to clear my throat. "Uh … maybe Joe and I should go find our own tree and give you two some privacy. Want us to take Daisy?"

Jed burst into laughter. "I think she's safe with us. We'll keep it PG."

Shaking his head with a grin, Joe then nodded toward the opposite direction. "Rose, what do you say we head over there?"

"Good idea."

We started walking in the opposite direction, and Joe fell into step beside me. "Got a particular kind of tree in mind?"

I shrugged. "Not really. We don't have a lot of space in the living room, so something not too bare but not too fat either."

He wrapped his free arm around my shoulder. "Now you sound like Goldilocks."

"Too bad I don't like porridge."

Since we weren't nearly as picky as Neely Kate, it only took us about thirty seconds to find a tree we agreed on.

"What do you think, Hopey?" Joe asked her as he pointed to it. "It's a pretty good tree for your first one, don't ya think?"

Hope looked up at him and waved her arms, excited that he was giving her attention.

Joe laughed as he squatted next to the tree with the saw. "I'll take that as a yes."

I glanced back at Jed and Neely Kate. Jed was swinging the ax at the tree trunk while Neely Kate watched his every move. "I bet you're wishing you had your own ax now."

"Nope, I'm more comfortable with a saw." I believed him after all his home improvement projects.

He sawed away at the trunk, while I squatted next to the stroller and told Hope what her daddy was doing.

It was a warm day for Christmas tree chopping, but it was better than being cold, and I enjoyed people watching as much as I enjoyed watching Joe make quick work of cutting down the tree. There were a lot of families at the tree farm. Some were enthusiastic about the excursion, but others had reluctant members in their group. Particularly, a family with a teenage girl and two younger siblings. The teenager spent most of her time on her phone until her father took it away and told her she was there to spend time with her family, not text her friends.

I wondered if Ashley and Hope would be like that someday. I supposed it was part of nature's way of making kids leave the nest, but I hoped they'd still love being with us.

One of the wagons was making its way up the hill to pick up customers and their trees, and I could see at least two families who looked ready to load up theirs.

"If we hurry, we might be able to get on this wagon," I said. "Unless you want to drag that tree back to the parking lot."

"Yeah," he grunted. "I'll pass." He put a little extra effort into sawing and the tree fell a few seconds later.

Joe set the saw on the ground as he lifted the tree, holding it upright at his side. I pulled my phone out of my jeans pocket and took a photo. "Do you feel like a lumberjack?"

He grinned. "I feel like a thirty-year-old guy pretending to be a lumberjack. I suspect I'll be sore tomorrow."

I laughed then bent to pull Hope out of the stroller. "Let's get a picture with Hope. Can you hold the tree upright *and* your daughter?"

He reached out his free arm and wriggled his fingers at me. "Bring her here."

I handed her to him, then stood back and took several photos, trying to get her to look at me, but she kept reaching up and grabbing Joe's ear. He couldn't stop laughing as he tried to convince her to look at Mommy, but she was more interested in him.

After we realized that was the best we were going to get, I walked over to them, held up my phone, and took a few selfies.

The wagon was approaching, so Joe handed Hope back to me and flagged them down. The driver, who was wearing a dirty

Santa hat, hopped out and helped load the tree in the back, then Joe collapsed the stroller and loaded it too. The two families were already on the wagon, and the teenage girl sat with her arms crossed over her chest, her lips pressed into a thin line.

We got in and rode the short distance to Jed and Neely Kate, and after they got their tree on board, the driver declared the wagon was full and headed back to the entrance. Joe narrated everything we saw to Hope who kept grabbing at his face, and my heart felt close to bursting.

The wagon rocked and bounced down the hill then stopped next to a sign that said *Christmas Tree Lane*. The lane was only about twenty feet long and six feet wide, with the shed at the entrance on the right, and several canopied tents scattered on the left. Christmas lights glowed overhead, attached to tall poles. Animatronics and inflatables lined the lane, but I could see the food truck farther down and at the end was a portable shed with a sign that read *Santa's Workshop*.

The driver turned around on his seat and patted his belly. "Ho, ho, ho. You've reached the North Pole and the end of your journey. Get your photos taken with Rudolph and Santa, while I take your tree up to the office to be wrapped up. The line for your photos is to the left."

Sure enough, on the left, past the inflatable angel, was a photo backdrop of snowy mountains. A four-foot-tall plastic Rudolph stood on one side with a family standing next to it. The father pretended to be feeding the reindeer his hat. Three more families stood in line, waiting their turn.

"Come on, Jed," Neely Kate said, moving to the end of the wagon. "Let's get in line."

Jed started to say something but then stopped and grinned. "Whatever you want, NK."

Joe glanced at the plastic reindeer, then tilted his head and pursed his lips. "Um … I think I'll go to the front office with the trees. You know, to make sure we get the tree we cut down."

"Good idea," I said a little too quickly. "Hope and I'll go with you."

"What?" Neely Kate said. "You can't go, Rose! Hope has to get a photo with Rudolph." Then she added, "But it makes sense for Joe to go. Rose, if you don't want to be alone in your photo, we can take one with you."

I didn't want to be in *any* photo with a plastic recreation of Rudolph that looked like it had been stored in a barn for fifty years, but I wasn't going to say so. For some reason, this was important to Neely Kate, and I was sure it was something other than her "Perfect Christmas" wish. But making such a big deal over a photo with a plastic reindeer seemed odd. This was further proof something big was eating at her. So, I smiled, and said, "Sounds good."

But I gave Joe the evil eye as the wagon pulled away.

Of course, he just laughed.

Chapter Five

Neely Kate

I felt a little foolish insisting Rose and Hope stay with us. I really *did* want a photo of my family, but Rose didn't need to be here, especially since Joe was going up to handle the trees. Yet, something deep inside said I needed her here. Maybe it was the panic roiling in my gut.

I'd spent all last night and today letting Carter's news fester inside me. If I thought I was panicked last night, it was even worse in the light of day. For most of the day, I'd convinced myself that Carter was only speculating—he didn't know anything for certain, but then when I least expected it, a fresh wave of terror would wash over me, making me feel like I was drowning. Having Rose and Joe with us made everything seem more normal, like Carter's news was just a bad dream. Being alone with Jed only made the fear worse.

But Jed was no fool. He knew something was up, and he'd asked me several times if I was okay. I'd tried to assure him without outright lying, but he knew me well enough to know I wasn't acting like myself.

I couldn't lose Jed. I just couldn't. I'd finally gotten the family I'd yearned for. I couldn't lose it all now.

So, I was desperate to keep Rose with me as long as possible, because ever since she and Joe had gotten here, I hadn't been so scared. Like everything was going to be okay.

She gave me a strange look as we got in line for our photos. She knew I was off today and I'd all but confirmed it earlier, so I offered her a weak smile, then turned to Daisy, who was back in Jed's arms. I told Daisy she was gonna get her photo taken with Rudolph, and then with Santa, and wasn't she excited? She cooed in response, and I grabbed her tiny hand in mine and thanked God for the billionth time for letting me have the blessing and honor of being her mommy.

What if Jed went to prison and I became a single mother, just like my own mother had been? Would I turn out like her too?

A sharp spike of fear shot through me and my body literally jerked.

Jed's forehead creased as worry filled his eyes. "I know I've asked a million times today, NK, but are you okay?"

"I'm fine," I lied, hating that I was lying, then I added, "I just have a headache." Which was true. It felt like tiny elves were pounding away in a workshop in my head.

"Do you want to go sit down?" Jed asked, pointing to the other side of the lane. "You can sit on that bench by the hot chocolate stand over there, then come back over when it's our turn."

"I'm fine," I said with a small laugh. "It's nothin'. I'd rather be here with you guys. Besides, we're next in line."

I had to admit that the teenage boy taking the photos with a digital camera seemed to be taking his time helping the people in front of us get set up for their shoot.

The family consisted of a man and a woman and three kids who looked like they were between the ages of two and six. The father tried to set the smallest kid on the back of the reindeer, and the photographer's eyes widened.

"Don't do that, sir!" he shouted, as the middle of the reindeer began to sag even more.

The father jumped back as though a monster was going to crash out of the plastic decoration, and in his haste, he left his child on the reindeer's back.

The mother had been sitting on a hay bale with the middle child on her lap, but she jumped to her feet, flinging the child onto the ground as she reached over to grab the toddler. The child on the ground began to cry, so now two of the three children were wailing. The oldest child stood behind the hay bale looking bored, making me wonder if this was a frequent happening in their household, although, I had to admit I hadn't seen this reindeer at the hardware store or Walmart.

"What were you *thinkin'*, Ron?" the woman screeched, not that I blamed her for being irate. He had abandoned his child in fear of his own safety.

"I … uh …" Ron stammered.

"That's the problem, you don't *think*, now, do ya?" She turned her ire to the photographer who was staring at them, looking stunned. "What are *you* lookin' at?"

The teenager grimaced as his face turned the color of a ripe tomato. "Sorry, ma'am, but I have to look at you to take the photo."

"Do we look like we're ready to take our photo?" she demanded.

"No, ma'am." Then the teenager rushed over to help the middle child who was still on her hands and knees in the fake snow scattered around the bale.

"Don't worry, Daisy," Jed murmured under his breath. "*I'd never let anything happen to you.*"

"He better not call *Neely Kate* ma'am," Rose said, also under her breath.

Jed let out a snicker, but I ignored them both. Sure, I was

known to get a little heated when called ma'am, but the family in front of us was causing enough drama on their own.

The photographer hurriedly got the family situated and didn't even bother to wait for the kids to stop crying. He just snapped a few photos then turned to us with pleading eyes. *"Next!"*

Jed and I moved over to the hay bale, and the photographer had Jed sit down with Daisy on his lap and me stand behind them and to the side, next to the reindeer that looked like a pinata that was only a couple of swings from busting open and spilling its contents onto the stuffing-covered ground.

The photographer still looked frazzled from the previous family, but he still spent several seconds trying to get Daisy to smile. I wasn't surprised she wasn't smiling. She was typically wary of strangers, but Rose moved next to him, calling Daisy's name. Daisy looked up at her and Rose began to make silly faces. Seconds later, Daisy giggled and the photographer got several photos.

"Next!" he called out, sounding weary. "Y'all can move to your left."

"Oh," I said, motioning to Rose. "We're gonna stay and have our friend join us."

Rose grimaced. "You don't have to do that. We don't need one."

"Come on. Jed, you get up and stand behind the bale, and Rose and I will sit with the babies."

Jed looked like he wanted to protest, but he was a good husband and did as I said as Rose walked over and reluctantly sat on the hay bale, next to Rudolph. I sat down too and noticed Hope squirming on Rose's lap, her little hands reaching up to try and touch the reindeer's faded red—now pale pink—nose. I supposed it was a distraction to her, given she was merely inches away from it.

Rose was trying to hold her still while the cameraman shook a bell. "Little baby, look over here."

But Hope was even more determined to touch the nose, and threw her head back into Rose's chest and practically launched herself at the reindeer.

Rose nearly lost her grip on Hope, but the baby got enough space to grab the reindeer's nose in both hands. Rose pulled her back while Hope still held on, and when Rose gave a hard yank, Hope let go and the reindeer toppled on to its side, the middle splitting in half.

The crowd let out cries of surprise. A kid called out "Cool!" while a few more began to cry.

Rose bolted upright. "I am so sorry!"

"You broke the reindeer," the photographer said in dismay as he moved toward it.

"We should just go," Rose said, propping Hope on her hip.

"We didn't get your photo taken yet," I protested.

"What do you want us to do?" Jed asked with a grin. "Should I put my foot on its rump and look like I brought it down with a machete like in those safari photos?"

I gasped. "Don't even suggest such a thing."

The teenager was still looking at the plastic pieces. "I wonder if I can put it back together with duct tape."

"Duct tape has a multitude of uses," I said. "That's not a bad idea." But the boy gave me a dark look, so I quickly followed Rose who had already bolted a good ten feet away.

"Rose, hold up," I called after her.

She slowed down and when I caught up, her face was red with embarrassment.

"It wasn't your fault," I assured her.

"She's right," Jed said. "Hope did the thing a favor by putting it out of its misery."

"Jed," I reprimanded him.

Jed shrugged. "Well, she did. That thing looked like it should have been put out to pasture decades ago. I'm surprised a few families of mice didn't come scurrying out when it broke in half."

Rose looked up at him and the corners of her mouth lifted into the hint of a smile before she said, "It's not funny."

"But, it kind of is," Jed said.

"He's right," I conceded. "It is funny."

Rose took a breath then looked around. "Where's Joe? I'm ready to get out of here."

"You can't go yet," I said as the panic started to reignite. Even the disaster that had happened behind us distracted me from the cloud hanging over me. "You didn't get your photo!"

"No offense," she said, "but it looks like they really are putting that poor reindeer back together with duct tape, and I don't need a photo of that thing in my house. It'll give Hope nightmares."

She had a point. The kid had gotten a roll of silver tape, and was struggling to hold up both ends of the plastic statue so he could tape it back together.

"I should go help," Rose said, looking like she was none too eager to do so. "It is my fault, after all."

"Nonsense," Jed countered. "If it hadn't happened with Hope, it would have happened with the next kid who tried to sit on its back, and they might have gotten hurt. You saved a kid from injury."

Rose snorted. "That thing is three feet off the ground. The worst that could happen is they'd get scraped up by the plastic."

"But think of the emotional damage," I said. "Something like that could ruin Christmas for a kid. Can you imagine a small child thinking they killed Rudolph?" I gave her a pointed look. "You did a public service."

Rose shook her head, making it obvious she wasn't buying it. "I'm still gonna go anyway. Before we get banned from Ned's tree lot."

I waved my hand. "They'd likely forget and let you back next year. You've been banned from the Piggly Wiggly multiple times and they always let you back."

She didn't argue, because she knew I was right.

Jed patted Rose's arm. "How about I go see if Joe's still dealing with the trees?"

Relief washed over her face. "Thank Jed."

I watched him walk toward the front of the lot, and I tried to figure out a way to keep Rose from leaving. "You still need a photo," I said, "so let's go see Santa."

Rose made a face. "Hope saw Santa in Little Rock last weekend with Ashley and Mikey," she said, then paused. "It did *not* go well."

She'd said their Santa trip had been a disaster, but hadn't elaborated. "Did she cry?" I asked.

She hesitated. "Something like that."

"Well, don't you think it would be cute to get photos of the two baby cousins together? Who cares if she cries. We can laugh about it years from now."

"So, you're encouraging me to let my baby cry?" she said with a grin.

"Well, of course not. I'm hoping she'll be distracted by Daisy and *won't* cry. Then you'll get an even better picture."

Rose took a deep breath and glanced to the front of the lot where Joe had gone to take care of the trees. There was still no sign of him. "I really wish Mike's parents would have let the kids come," she said. "Joe asked them yesterday, but Mike's dad hung up on him."

I bounced Daisy on my hip. "I can't believe they're being so spiteful. They're only hurtin' the kids." Then I realized what she wasn't saying. "You want them in the Santa photo too."

Her eyes turned glassy. "I don't want them to feel left out."

"I understand," I said, and I did. I knew what it had been like on the outside of the Rivers family, wishing I was in the center. "But we can tell them that we had the babies take a photo together. Mikey won't care and Ashley will think they're cute."

"True," she said, but the frown on her face proved she wasn't convinced.

"I understand if you don't want to do it," I said, realizing I was being selfish. "I didn't mean to push."

She turned to me and studied my face. "What's goin' on with you today? I mean, I know you want this Christmas season to be perfect since it's your first with Daisy, but you seem a little manic about it. You said you'd tell me what was bothering you later. Can you tell me now?"

Tears sprung to my eyes. I wanted to tell her—I needed to tell her, but it felt like a betrayal to tell Rose before I told Jed. Still, this was too big to deal with on my own.

Rose put a hand on my arm. "You can tell me *anything*, Neely Kate. Lord knows I've told you a million things that have bothered me in the past." A warm grin tipped up the corners of her mouth.

I glanced toward the parking lot, looking to see if Jed was within earshot. I definitely didn't want him walking up and overhearing. "You can't tell anyone—especially Joe," I said. "I haven't even told Jed yet."

Her eyes widened slightly. "Okay. I promise."

I glanced at the crowd around us and pulled her over next to an inflatable snowflake. When I was sure no one would overhear us, I lowered my voice and leaned in close. "I saw Carter Hale at Nicholson's Farm Supply last night."

"Okay…" she said hesitantly.

"I think he followed me there so he could tell me something important."

Her forehead furrowed with confusion. "Why wouldn't he just call or drop by the office?"

"I suspect he didn't want to tell me on a phone call in case it was being tapped, and I also suspect he wanted to tell me on my own and let me decide what to do with the information."

"You mean, he was worried I'd be there." Her face paled. "Was it about James?"

I was surprised at the niggle of irritation that burned in my chest. "Not everything is about Skeeter Malcolm," I snapped more forcefully than I'd meant.

Her cheeks flushed as contrition filled her eyes. "I'm sorry, Neely Kate. That was incredibly narcissistic of me."

I shook my head as I felt the familiar sting of unshed tears. "No. *I'm* sorry. Of course you'd think that. Skeeter and Carter are practically married at hip."

A half-hearted grin spread across her face. "I think it's *joined* at the hip."

"Whatever," I said with a wave. "That's not the point." I stopped and looked around again then turned back to her. "He was there about Jed."

Her brow shot up. "Jed!" she whisper-shouted. "What about him?"

"Carter said the Feds are gonna question him after the first of the year. He wanted to warn me so that we could get a good attorney and prepare for it."

Rose's face paled and she squeezed my hand. "Oh, Neely Kate!"

"I know." I brushed a tear away.

"Are they questioning him about ..." She grimaced. "You know who?"

I snorted. "You can say his name. And yeah, I think so. Carter thinks they're hoping to build a stronger case to convict Skeeter." A lump clogged my throat. "What if Jed has to incriminate himself?"

A fierce look washed over her face. "Carter's right. You need an attorney. Is he gonna help Jed?"

"No, he said he can't. It would look bad, not that Jed would probably want him to anyway. Carter said he tried to call Jed to tell him, but he'd blocked his number. Carter suggested I ask

Mason for recommendations, because he thinks the questioning will take place in Little Rock."

"Mason?" She drew in a breath and let it out. "Oh, Neely Kate, I'm so, so sorry."

Tears streamed down my cheeks. "I can't lose him, Rose. I just can't."

She pulled me into a sideways hug, so we didn't smash our babies. "You *won't*. Mason will know someone who will get him out of this."

"Carter couldn't get Skeeter out of his mess, and even Mason says that Carter's good. *Really* good."

"Well," she said with a sigh. "I think Carter *had* helped him, and James threw it all away." She dropped her gaze to Hope, then kissed her head as tears filled her eyes.

"You can't feel guilty about that, Rose," I said insistently.

She nodded, but didn't look convinced, but then she forced a smile. "I have faith that Mason can help. The real question is why you're confiding in me and not telling Jed."

"I wanted this Christmas to be perfect, and if we have this hanging over our heads…"

"It's already hanging over *your* head," she said, squeezing my arm. "Besides, Jed has the right to know."

I swiped a tear from my cheek. "I know he does. And I'll tell him. Just let me have this weekend."

"Okay." She hugged me again, holding me tight until Hope began to squirm. "But you *have* to tell him next week. Joe and I will be happy to watch Daisy when you interview attorneys in Little Rock."

"Little Rock?" I heard Joe say behind me. "Are you talking about our trip last weekend?"

Rose pulled away, but before either of us could answer, Jed said, "I thought you were supposed to be standing in line to see Santa."

"You're gonna let Hope see Santa?" Joe said in amused disbelief. "After what happened last weekend? I haven't bought that umbrella insurance yet, so I'm not sure we should risk it."

Eager to turn attention away from my conversation with Rose, I asked, "What happened last weekend?"

Joe's eyes lit up. "I can't believe Rose didn't tell you. Hope was terrified of Santa, and when he leaned down to talk to her, she head-butted him in the face and busted his nose."

"What?" I said, turning to Rose in shock. "Why didn't you tell me?"

She grimaced. "It's not exactly something to be proud of."

"His nose started gushing blood," Joe said. "It looked like a crime scene. Ashley freaked out—as did all the kids waiting in line—but Mikey thought Hope was pretty badass."

Jed burst into laughter, choking out, "That's because she is. Maybe we should start calling her slugger."

"Do *not* call her slugger," Rose hissed. "It was awful. Over a dozen kids thought our sweet baby killed Santa." She gave me an apologetic look. "So... I think we'll skip another Santa visit." She glanced up at the sky. "In fact, it looks like some storm clouds are rolling in, so maybe we should get home before the rain hits."

"I'm gonna agree with my wife on that one," Joe said, lifting Hope out of Rose's arms. "We got the trees all paid for. I just need to pull up the truck and load it up." He turned to Jed. "You need help getting your tree home?"

"We got it covered."

I felt something wet hit my hand and realized it was a raindrop.

"Right on cue," Rose said, then she pulled me into a hug and whispered in my ear, "I'm just a phone call or text away if you need me."

I squeezed her back then pulled away. "Get goin' before you get soaked." I watched her and Joe hurry to the parking lot, as Jed said, "You want to wait in line to see Santa? I can get an umbrella, so you and Daisy don't get wet."

I shook my head, most of my Christmas spirit fading. Now that my buffer of Rose and Joe were gone, all I had left was my fear and the giant chasm of my lie of omission. I knew I should tell him, but I just couldn't do it. Not yet.

I had someone else I needed to talk to first, because I knew Jed's pride would keep him from doing it.

I needed to have a face-to-face chat with Skeeter Malcolm.

Chapter Six

Rose

After we loaded the Christmas tree into the truck bed, Joe turned on Christmas songs and started singing, much to Hope's delight. She couldn't see him in her rear-facing car seat, but she knew his voice and cooed along with him. When he realized she loved *Jingle Bells*, he put the song on repeat.

"Again?" I asked sarcastically.

He shot me a grin. "Our daughter loves it. How can I deny her?"

"You know that song's gonna be stuck in my head now."

His eyes lit up with mischief. "Good thing you love me."

"Guilty as charged."

We drove through a light drizzle all the way home, so when Joe pulled up in front of our house, he told me to take Hope inside and he'd bring in the tree.

After I unlocked the door, I let Muffy out to potty and greet Joe, then headed to the kitchen to make some hot chocolate. I knew Hope would want to nurse soon, so I set her in the highchair and gave her a handful of Cheerios to keep her occupied as I started putting the ingredients for the hot chocolate in a pan.

A few minutes later, the front door opened and Joe called out, "Where's the Christmas tree stand?"

"In the corner in front of the window," I hollered back. I glanced over at Hope who was in deep concentration, trying to grab cereal pieces with her chubby fist, so I grabbed a plastic pitcher and filled it with water so it would be ready once Joe had the tree in the stand.

I moved to the doorway to the living room. The tree was still bound and lying on its side in the middle of the floor. Joe was kneeling next to the trunk, screwing the tree stand into the trunk.

"Do you need help?" I asked.

"Maybe in a minute," he said, not looking up. "I might need you to hold it up after I get it upright so I can make sure it's standing up straight."

"Sure. I've started some hot chocolate, and I'm tryin' to figure out what to make for dinner."

He turned his head to look up at me. "The hot chocolate sounds good, and how about we go out for dinner? We can try out the new Chinese place."

"I've been wanting to try that place out."

He grinned. "I know."

I turned to head back into the kitchen when a knock at the front door stopped me in my tracks.

Joe sat upright. "Are we expecting anyone?"

"Not that I know of," I said, slightly worried. We rarely got unannounced visitors, and when we had in the past, they had usually been unwelcome visitors. But I realized who was likely at the door. "It's probably Neely Kate here to pick up the platform for her tree."

He made a face. "I forgot all about that."

"That's understandable. None of us mentioned it since we cut the trees down." I grinned. "But you know Neely Kate. Once she sets her mind on something, she won't let it go. I'll get the door."

Still, he looked uncertain, and I understood why. Months ago, any number of dangerous people could have been knocking on our door.

"It's okay." I turned around to check on Hope. Most of the Cheerios were still on the tray and she looked like she was getting frustrated. I scooped her out of the seat and popped a piece of cereal in her mouth as I headed for the front door.

There was another knock as I reached for the handle. When I opened the door, it wasn't Neely Kate or Jed. Instead, an older woman had her hand lifted, ready to knock again.

She wore brown dress pants and a cream-colored silky shirt with a bow tied at the side of her neck. She had shoulder-length dark hair that was cut in a bob. Crow's feet cracked her previously perfect porcelain skin. Irritation covered her face as her gaze landed on me, but then it was quickly replaced by a bright smile.

She looked familiar, but she'd aged since the last time I'd seen her, so it took me a few seconds to realize who was standing at our door. What was she doing here? How had she found us?

"Rose," Joe said behind me. "Who is it?"

The woman's smile spread at the sound of Joe's voice, and she tried to peer past me.

"Joe," I said, my voice coming out in a squeak. I wasn't sure how he was going to react to seeing her. This woman had hurt him time and time again, and for a split second, I wondered if I could send her away and save him from this.

But he was already on his feet, coming up behind me, and I heard him gasp in shock.

"Now, Joe," the woman said with a pout. "You look like you've seen the ghost of Christmas past. Is that any way to greet your mother?"

Chapter Seven

Rose

Joe stood behind me in silence for several seconds.

"Aren't you gonna invite me in?" Betsy Simmons asked, her gaze rising to Joe.

I felt him stiffen behind me.

"Mother," he said, his voice tight. "What are you doing here?"

She pressed her hand to her chest as a careful look of dismay spread across her face. "How can you ask me that? I'm your *mother.*" A diamond ring on her right hand glittered in the sunlight. Considering the FBI had confiscated all of the Simmons property after J.R. Simmons' death, I was surprised to see she still owned something so expensive.

"Why are you here?" he repeated, his voice devoid of emotion.

"Well…" Her hand dropped to her side. "I heard you had a baby, and since you didn't bother to let me know I'm a grandmother, I decided I had to come see him for myself." She lifted her hand and reached for Hope. "And here he is."

"Here *she* is," Joe said, stepping in front of me and blocking his mother's access to our daughter. "She's your grand*daughter.* But now you've seen her. Mission accomplished. You can go."

Something in me bristled at his tone, but I fought the urge to intervene. Joe had been to hell and back for most of his life.

While his father had been the puppet master, his mother had never done anything to intervene. This was *Joe's* mother, and I needed to follow his lead.

"Are you really not going to let me in?" she asked in genteel outrage. "After I came all this way?"

"No one asked you to come," Joe said, "and didn't you always teach us to never drop into someone's home unexpected? You should have called first."

"Joe," his mother's voice softened. "I know we parted on bad terms when I left—"

"You mean how you called me every name in the book when the FBI showed up to confiscate everything we owned, and you took off and left me there to deal with it?" He tilted his head. "Seems like you disowned me, if I remember correctly."

She sighed. "Tensions were high that day. We both said things I'm sure we regret."

"No," Joe said calmly. "I don't have any regrets."

Mrs. Simmons was quiet for a few seconds. "Well," she said, her voice softer still. "I realize I've let time get away from me, and I'll also admit, I let my pride get in the way. I'd like to think you did too."

"Pride had nothing to do with me pretending that you no longer existed." His voice sounded strained on the last two words, the only sign she was getting to him.

"Okay," she said, her voice still soft. "Maybe it was only my pride. I should have reached out sooner, but we've let this go on far too long. We're family. We need each other."

"Family?" he asked with a bitter laugh. "Where were you when I buried your *daughter*?"

She winced, but to my amazement, she didn't show any signs of anger. "Mistakes were made."

Joe laughed again. "Mistakes were made," he mocked. "You think?"

I put my hand on Joe's shoulder to let him know I was there supporting him. He wasn't facing her alone.

Joe drew in a deep breath, then said, "I don't have any money, Mother."

Her body stiffened. "Who said I was here for money?"

I could see hurt washing over her face, but I reminded myself that his mother was the consummate actress who had let money rule her life. When she'd been kicked out of her house, she'd gone to live with her parents, and I hadn't heard anything else about what had happened to her. But her parents were simple people who didn't have money of their own, and Betsy had grown used to living in a large home with staff. It would be surprising if she *wasn't* here for money.

"Joe," she chastised gently as though he were being an unreasonable child. "Don't be crass. I'm your *mother*. I'm here because I want to see you and meet my grandchild." Then a hint of reprimand edged into her voice. "If you would have reached out to me *first*, then I wouldn't be here unannounced."

Joe's shoulders rose and fell as his breathing hitched up.

She looked past Joe, and her steely eyes landed on me. "Rose, I would love a chance to get to know you and meet my granddaughter. If you'll just let me in, I'm sure we can talk through these hurt feelings."

I didn't respond, because this was Joe's decision, not mine. But I had to admit that part of me wanted to believe her. Did she know that Joe's hurt feelings went far deeper than angry words spoken the last time they'd seen each other? That he still hurt from years of neglect and being constantly told that he wasn't enough?

"Well?" she asked. "It's rude to leave a person standing out on the porch in the cold, Joseph. I raised you better than that."

Joe clenched his fists at his sides, the first hint of anger. "*You* raised me? Roberta, *the housekeeper*, raised me. Not you and *definitely* not my father."

A tight smile lifted her lips, and she clasped her hands at her waist. "Joe…"

"Mother, you of all people know *rude*," Joe said bluntly. "You were the queen of it, lording over your friends and icing out the ones who dared to stand up to you." He crossed his arms over his chest. "And you can't say you're standing out in the cold. It's sixty-five degrees outside."

"But it's raining," she protested.

"You're standing on a covered porch," he said dryly.

Betsy pushed out a long sigh, then lifted her clasped hand up to her chest as though she was praying. "I will admit that mistakes were made," she said, her voice breaking. "But it's time to move past them, Joe. I want to have a relationship with you. I want to know my grandchild."

"Mistakes *were* made," Joe said in a flat tone. "But I'm curious what you think those mistakes *are*."

His mother's eyes widened slightly, and she drew a breath, hesitating.

"Yeah," Joe said in disgust. "That's what I thought. I don't know why you're here, and frankly, I don't care. I don't have any interest in seeing you, and you sure as hell aren't coming anywhere near my daughter. So, go back to the rock you crawled out from under." Then he slammed the door in her face.

He spun around to face me, his jaw clenched as his breath came in rapid bursts.

My heart ached for him. "Joe. Are you okay?"

He silently shook his head and stalked back over to the tree still lying on the floor.

I stepped over to the living room window and peered through the sheer curtains. Joe's mother had descended the porch steps and was looking back at the house. She looked lost as she studied the house for a few moments, then she climbed into an older sedan. She backed up and headed back to the county road.

"Well…" Joe finally said, shoving the tree trunk into the tree stand. "Go ahead and say it."

"Say what?" I asked, holding Hope close.

"You probably think I'm a terrible person for slamming the door in her face and not hearing her out."

"I would *never* say that, Joe."

"But you're thinkin' it."

I shook my head, then walked over and sat on the floor next to him, placing a hand on his shoulder. "No, Joe. You have every right to feel the way you feel."

He leaned his head into my arm and closed his eyes. "Why do I think there's a but in there?"

"There's no but. Her showing up on our front porch out of the blue had to be a shock. You've told me how terrible she was to you after your father died, not to mention all the years before that. And don't forget I met her when we were dating. She wasn't exactly sweetness and light to me."

He reached a hand up and covered mine with his own. "But *you* would give her a chance."

"I don't know," I said honestly. "Maybe. Maybe not. If my momma showed up at the door, would I give her the time of day? I'm not so sure."

"I would hope you wouldn't give your mother the time of day, considering she's been dead for two years and she'd be a zombie," he teased.

"True," I said with a soft grin. "But even if she weren't a zombie, I'm not sure what I'd do."

"I do," he said, sounding defeated. "You would have let her in."

Would I? I considered it a moment. "The last words I spoke to my mother were said in anger," I said. "I don't regret them because they were a long time comin'. But if she showed up, I'm not so sure I'd let her in. Not without letting her know I was a different person now, and she couldn't treat me the way she used to when she was alive, or I'd kick her out."

"See? You'd see her, you'd just lay ground rules first."

I hesitated. "I suppose I would see her, but only because I'm a different person now. I think I'd need to prove to myself that she can't hurt me anymore." I squeezed his shoulder. "You don't need to prove anything to anyone, Joe. If you never want to see her again, then that's okay. No one can fault you for that."

His voice broke. "She didn't even come to Kate's memorial service."

While his sister had always been a wild card and had done many unscrupulous things, she'd gone off the deep end when she'd kidnapped Hope, plotted to kill me, then planned to give my baby to Neely Kate. Kate had been killed in the end, and while Joe had hated the things she'd done, he'd blamed his parents for screwing her up.

When Betsy hadn't claimed Kate's body, Joe held a private service for her. He'd sent word through his grandparents with details about the service, but neither they nor Betsy had come. There had only been three people at the service—Joe, Neely Kate, and Jed (I couldn't bring myself to go), and Betsy's absence had hurt Joe more than he'd let on, even if Neely Kate had been relieved.

"I know," I said. "I'm so sorry. Nothin' about this is easy. I don't blame you for sending your mom away, and if you never speak to her again, I'll stand by that decision." I hesitated. "If I'm honest, I'm not sure I want her around Hope and the kids, but I'll respect your wishes no matter what you decide."

He turned to face me, still kneeling and holding his hand over mine on his shoulder. "I love you, Rose."

I leaned over and kissed him, holding Hope to my chest. "I love you too."

Chapter Eight

Neely Kate

Jed and I got the Christmas tree in the stand and the lights wrapped around the branches while Daisy took her nap, but we decided to hold off on putting the ornaments on until we got the platform. The tree was pretty with just the lights, and Daisy was mesmerized. Jed teased me that she was just like her mother, taken in by sparkly lights.

On Sunday morning, Joe brought over a foot-tall platform, and he helped Jed get the tree set up on it. Before he left, he told us that his mother had shown up on their doorstep after they'd gotten home from the Christmas tree farm, and he'd sent her away.

My stomach twisted. Joe's mother hated me. I couldn't blame her, given that I was physical proof her husband had cheated on her, but I reminded myself that she had no power over me. Still, I felt relieved that Joe didn't want to see her, even if it was selfish of me.

"What did she want?" Jed asked.

"She claimed she wanted to reconnect with me and to have a relationship with her granddaughter—who she thought was a grandson until we corrected her," he said in disgust. "But I'm not buying it for a minute."

"Then what do you think she wanted?" Jed asked.

"Hell if I know."

"You should find out," I said quietly.

He turned to me in surprise. "Why?"

"Because if my mother showed up on my doorstep, I'd want to know. I'd hate her, and I'd probably send her away at first too, but ultimately, I'd want to know why she went to the trouble of coming all this way to see me."

"But she didn't even come to Kate's funeral," he said, his voice breaking. "Her own daughter."

"I know," I said past the lump in my throat. It had killed Joe at the time, and he'd vowed he was done with her. "She's a selfish bitch, but I'd still want to know."

Joe's eyes grew haunted.

"How did Rose take it?" Jed asked.

"Pretty well, considering she was the one to answer the door. She backs my decision, and she thinks I handled the whole situation well; however, she said if her mother showed up, she'd ultimately want to talk to her."

"So, what are you going to do?" Jed asked.

Joe ran a hand over his head. "I don't know, but last night while I was in bed, unable to sleep, Rose told me I can take my time to figure it out. There's no hurry to make a decision."

"Typical Rose answer," I said with a soft smile. "Just because your mother decided now was the time to drop into your life, doesn't mean it's the right time for *you*."

"Yeah."

"Let her stew," I said. "You've got plenty of time to sort it out."

"Unless she's dyin'," Jed said. "Then you might not."

I swatted his thick bicep. "Hush your mouth. I suspect that self-centered woman would have led with that."

The hint of a grin cracked Joe's serious expression. "You're right."

He left soon after that, and Jed and I decorated the tree during

Daisy's next nap. The FBI threat still hung over my head, no matter how much I tried to ignore it. Jed knew something was bothering me, and he asked a few times if I was okay, but he finally kissed me and said he would stop pestering me, that he knew I'd tell him when I was ready.

Which made me feel even more guilty for keeping it from him.

But why was I keeping it from him? It was wrong. He had a right to know. Yet, I knew once I told him, our life wouldn't be the same until it was resolved. And I'd rather suffer with the uncertainty on my own than drag Jed into it and destroy any hope of a happy Christmas.

When Jed put Daisy down for her afternoon nap, I decided to get a jump start on my plan and I sent Carter a text.

I need to meet with you tomorrow

He sent a response back pretty quickly.

I already told you I can't help you

I know. This is about something else

He didn't respond for nearly a minute before he texted back.

When have I ever been able to refuse you anything? Be at my office at 9:00 sharp

THE NEXT MORNING, I got to the office a little after eight, still trying to figure out how to explain to Rose why I was leaving the office and walking across the square to Carter's office. There wouldn't be any hiding it from her. Our office had a direct line of sight to his.

But soon after I sat at my desk, Rose called and said that Mikey had come back from his grandparents' with a cold and a fever. She was going to stay home with him and try to work from home.

Typically, I didn't like being alone in the office—I didn't like being alone period—but this morning I was happy for it, despite the fact that my imagination was running wild with all the possible doomsday scenarios. Surely, there was a way to stop the FBI from questioning Jed. I just needed to get Carter to help me.

At 8:55, I locked up the office and headed across the square. I'd considered bringing Carter a coffee from the shop a few doors down to butter him up, but he took his coffee black, likely to match his soul. I wasn't gonna spend three dollars on a cup of coffee that wasn't loaded with sugar and milk.

A small Christmas tree was in front of the office window when I walked up. It took me by surprise because I'd never seen Carter decorate his office for the holidays before. I figured it had been done by his receptionist of the week.

Sure enough, I didn't recognize the woman sitting at the desk in the waiting room, and I wondered how she'd found the resources to decorate. I couldn't imagine Carter springing for them. The young girl looked up at me with a stern look that might have been more believable if she wasn't wearing her hair in low pigtails, making her look like she belonged in middle school, not behind the public-facing desk in Carter Hale, Attorney at Law's reception area.

"Do you have an appointment?" she asked, her mouth pursing.

I gave her a pointed look. "Does Carter have *any* appointments today?"

She glanced down at a planner on the desk and scanned it for several seconds before she lifted her gaze. "He has court in an hour, but other than that, no. *Nevertheless*, he's a very, very busy man. You'll need to make an appointment."

Carter was either paying her to say that or she was as clueless as she looked. "I'm sure Carter's busy all right," I said mockingly even as I realized he must have made our appointment at nine because of his court schedule. "Is he in his office?"

"Mr. Hale says I'm not supposed to let clients see him unless they have an appointment," she insisted.

"Then don't you worry your pretty little head," I said with a sarcastic smile. "I have an appointment with Carter at nine, so he'll be more than happy to see me."

"But it's not on the book," she said, tapping a long, blue-painted fingernail on the planner. "See?"

"Does he take the planner home with him on the weekends?"

She gave me a snide smile. "No, but he tells me *everything*, and he didn't tell me about this." I was pretty sure the innuendo in that sentence was purposeful. Did she think I was after Carter Hale? I nearly laughed, but then I sobered. Did that mean he was sleeping with her? He had to be nearly twice her age. Gross.

I propped a hand on my hip, quickly losing patience. "So are you going to check with him to see I have an appointment or not?"

Her lips pursed. "Not."

This was ridiculous and I wasn't in the mood to deal with her bullshit when my husband's freedom was on the line.

I walked around her desk and started down the hall toward Carter's office.

She jumped up from her desk and tried to run after me, shouting, "Mr. Hale is a very busy man! He can't see you without an appointment!"

I'd already told her I had one, so I didn't see the point of arguing with her.

Carter's door was shut, so I threw it open without even bothering to knock. "Is this the way you treat all your clients or is this just special for me?"

I felt a little bad when I saw that Carter was on the phone. He was sitting behind his massive wooden desk, leaning back in his leather office chair. He looked up with an exasperated expression, then said into the phone, "I'm gonna need to call you back." He hung up without waiting for a response.

The receptionist ran in behind me. "Mr. Hale! I am *so* sorry! I tried to stop her!"

He gave her a wry grin. "Don't worry, Samantha. When Miss Colson is determined to do something, there's no stopping her."

"That's *Mrs.* Carlisle." I shot him a glare. He knew I was married. Hell, he'd stalked me to the farm store to talk to me about my husband. Why couldn't he use my married name?

"Oh, yes, how could I forget?" he said wryly. "Mrs. Carlisle."

Samantha shot me a glance then turned back to Carter. "She said she had an appointment, but I said you would have told me if she had."

He nodded toward her. "Don't worry, Samantha. I've got it covered from here. Ms. *Carlisle* has a mind of her own." He turned his attention to me and waved to the two chairs in front of his desk. "Neely Kate, please come in. Samantha, shut the door behind you."

Samantha gave me another long look before she walked out, closing the door just as her boss had asked.

"Why didn't you just tell her I had an appointment?" I asked, my temper rising. "You let her think I just barged on in."

He steepled his fingers on his desk. "How many times have you barged in?"

"I didn't this time!"

He shrugged. "What did you need to see me about?"

I'd planned to sugar coat it and work my way to my big ask, but I didn't feel like playing any games right now. "I need to see Skeeter."

He stared at me like he hadn't understood.

"Can you—" I shook my head. "Scratch that, I'm not asking. Make the arrangements."

He stared at me for a moment longer. "Well, you do have lady balls, I'll give you that."

"I want to see him tomorrow."

He sat back in his seat, his eyes narrowing. "Why in the hell do you want to see Skeeter?"

"That's my business."

"He's not gonna help you."

"Who said I was gonna ask for his help?"

He made a face that suggested he thought I was a fool. "It doesn't take a genius to figure it out."

Okay, he had a point.

He shook his head. "You need to do as I said and find an attorney. What did Deveraux say? Did he give you any recommendations?"

"I haven't called Mason yet," I said, glancing down at my lap, then I lifted my gaze. "Other than Rose, I haven't told anyone."

His brow rose. "What do you mean you haven't told anyone? Not even your husband?"

"No."

He let out a sigh, then pinched the bridge of his nose for several seconds before dropping his hand and sitting back in his seat. Pity covered his face. "Going over to see Skeeter is a fool's errand, Neely Kate. First of all, I doubt he'd even see you. Second, I don't know what you expect him to do."

Tears stung my eyes. "Do you think he could tell them that Jed doesn't have anything to do with the Hardshaw Group?"

He pushed out a sigh. "That's a loaded question. We don't know that Skeeter will even be willing to talk to them. He sees Jed picking you over him as a betrayal."

My chest tightened. "I know."

"And even if he did tell them Jed was innocent, I'm not sure they'd believe him."

I drew in a deep breath, trying to push down my rising panic. "I have to try, Carter. I can't lose him."

Sympathy filled his eyes. "Neely Kate, your time would be better served by finding a good attorney who can advise Jed on what to say, and what not to say, when they question him."

"They want information on Skeeter, right?" I asked. "What if Jed promises not to tell them anything?"

His face turned to stone. "I cannot advise either you or your husband on how to answer questions posed by any law-enforcement agency," he said, his voice full of authority that I wasn't used to hearing. "That's why I told you to find him a hot shot attorney."

"But surely—"

His brow furrowed. "You know, I didn't have to warn you about the FBI, especially after Jed so callously turned his back on Skeeter."

That stoked my anger. "Jed didn't turn on him! Skeeter was the one who turned his back on Jed. Skeeter made Jed choose between the two of us. Why couldn't he have both?"

Carter pushed out a heavy sigh. "I think we both know that having someone you care about doesn't work very well in this line of business. They're a liability."

Rose was proof enough of that. Look at where Skeeter was now.

I shot him a glare. "So, Jed wasn't supposed to have a life?"

He pushed out another sigh. "This is a pointless discussion."

I lifted my chin in defiance. "If you won't take me to see him, I'll go on my own tomorrow."

He shook his head. "You'll never get in. Visitors' day is on the weekend, and even if you go, I suspect he won't agree to see you."

I stood. "I guess I'll take my chances."

"I'm not sure what you think Skeeter can do. He can't even help himself."

"I thought *you* were some hot shot attorney who can get anybody out of anything," I snapped.

"I can only help those who want to help themselves," he said in defeat.

Was Carter really claiming that Skeeter wasn't trying to help himself now? There was no question that he'd given up his immunity to save Hope and Rose. Did that mean he hadn't had a backup Plan B? I didn't believe that for a second. He always had a plan to make sure he ended up on top, which meant something was holding him back from enacting his plan.

I nearly gasped. Was Skeeter protecting someone else?

"Are you saying Skeeter is trying to help Jed?"

Carter made a face as he looked down at his desk. He studied a spot on his blotter for a few seconds before he lifted his head and looked me square in the eye. "You're asking me to break confidentiality with my client."

"I need to see him, Carter," I said softly. "Maybe there's a way Jed can help Skeeter."

"You must be having delusions of grandeur. I don't see how Jed could help him."

"Maybe not, but we won't know if we don't at least try."

"It's a waste of everyone's time."

"Carter. I'm begging you. Please take me to see him."

Shaking his head, he turned to the side and studied his University of Arkansas diplomas on the wall. "Damn, you sure are a persistent creature."

"You have no idea."

"Okay, fine," he said, but he didn't sound happy about it.

"Okay?" I asked in disbelief. "You'll take me to see him?"

"It'll take me a day or two to work it out, but yeah. I'll take you."

"Thank, Carter! Thank you!" I gushed. "You have no idea how much I appreciate this!"

"Don't get your hopes up," he said. "I suspect no good will come of this."

I was betting our futures that he was wrong.

Chapter Nine

Rose

By Monday night, Mikey was going stir crazy from staying home all day. His fever had broken the night before, but I'd kept him home so he'd be fever-free for twenty-four hours before going back to school.

He and Ashley had been out of sorts when Mike's parents had brought them home Sunday afternoon, but it wasn't uncommon for them to be quiet after a visit with their grandparents. Then, when Mikey wasn't excited about decorating the tree, I figured out pretty quickly that he was running a fever. Ashley confirmed that Mikey had been sick with a cold since Saturday night and Mike's parents had still made him go to church. I'd been furious and had wanted to call them, especially since they hadn't told us Mikey had been sick, but instead, I handed Hope to Joe and snuggled on the sofa with Mikey while we watched *Elf*, his favorite Christmas movie. After we finished the movie, Muffy snuggled with him as Ashley, Joe, and I decorated the tree. Hope sat in her bouncy seat, mesmerized by the lights.

On Monday morning, Joe took Ashley to school before he headed to Baton Rouge to get more lights, and I kept Hope home with me and Mikey. I didn't get much work done at home, but I was more worried that I couldn't be at the office to see Neely

Kate. When I'd called her in the morning to tell her Mikey was sick and we were staying home, she seemed okay, but when I asked if she'd talked to Jed, she'd told me she didn't feel like talking about it and quickly ended the call.

I still hadn't told Joe, even though I was dying to get his opinion, but it wasn't my information to share. I'd promised to keep it to myself.

Everything was back to normal on Tuesday. I took Hope to daycare after I dropped the kids off at school, then headed downtown to the office.

Neely Kate was already at her desk when I arrived. She looked up as I walked in and glanced down at my feet. "No Muffy today?"

I headed for my desk. "I figured she got enough peopling the last three days. Mikey pretty much squeezed the stuffing out of her Sunday night and yesterday while he was feeling bad, so I let her have some alone time to recover."

She chuckled. "She loved every minute of it, and you know it."

"True, but she didn't run to the door today to leave with us, so I let her make her own decision."

I sat down and booted up my computer, telling Neely Kate what little I had done the day before.

"Have you heard anything more from Joe's mom?" she asked.

"Not a thing."

"Do you think that means she accepted Joe's answer?"

Joe and I had discussed it the night before, and he'd confessed that while he was relieved she'd given up so easily, part of him was disappointed too.

"I know it's counterintuitive," he'd said as we lay in bed, me nestled into his side. "I don't want anything to do with her, but some small part of me wanted her to at least fight a little bit for me."

"That makes perfect sense," I'd said. "We all want our mothers to fight for us." We'd been talking about Joe and his mother, but I couldn't help wondering if Violet would be upset with me for not fighting harder to protect her kids. I didn't know what else to do, though. Mike's parents refused to listen to Joe or me, and the attorney said the judge likely wouldn't change the visitation schedule until Mike had either been exonerated or convicted.

But Neely Kate was watching me now with a worried look. "Are you okay?"

"Honestly?" I asked, sitting back in my seat. "No. I'm worried about Joe. I'm worried about the kids, and I'm worried about you and Jed."

She waved her hand. "Slow down and forget about me and Jed right now. Why are you worried about the kids? Is Mikey still not feeling well?"

I told her about the condition they'd come home in and how Mike's parents had taken the kids to church despite the fact Mikey was ill. "I don't know what to do about it," I confessed, close to tears.

She studied me for a long moment, before she said, "You've got to talk to Mike."

My eyes widened. "What?"

Nodding, she continued, "You have to go talk to him and convince him to think of the kids. Convince him that this shared custody isn't working out and that this isn't what Violet wanted. Tell him that his parents can see them once in a while, but not when they put their own needs over the kids, like they did this weekend. Because you know darn good and well, they only took him to church because, one, it's their main source of socializing, and two, they wanted to prove they had their grandkids. It's a one-upmanship for them, not because they actually want the kids."

I wasn't sure I agreed with that, but part of what she said felt true. They hated that I had partial custody, as though that meant they were deemed unfit, so they paraded the kids around whenever they had them, taking them to church and out for Sunday lunch.

"And if that doesn't convince him," she continued, "tell Mike to ask his kids what *they* want."

I grimaced. "I don't want to put them in that position. I don't want to make them choose."

"But what if they *want* to choose?"

I'd never considered their choice to be an option, mostly because our family attorney said it wasn't. She'd said they were too young to decide what they wanted, but were they? If they were miserable at their grandparents', shouldn't they have a say in whether they went there or not?

Neely Kate was right. While the courts didn't care what the kids wanted, surely Mike did.

"You're right," I said.

A grin of triumph spread across her face as she cupped her hand around her ear. "What was that?"

I groaned good-naturedly. "You're right, and I have no trouble admitting that you're right, so what's with the gloating?"

"I just like to hear it, is all," she said, giving me a smug grin.

"We got me sorted out, so what's going on with you and Jed? You refused to discuss it yesterday when I called. Does that mean you still haven't told him?"

She turned back to her computer. "I have something else in the works."

I narrowed my eyes. "What does that mean?"

A tight smile lifted the corner of her mouth. "I'll tell you after it's done."

"Why do I not like the sound of that?"

Her cell phone rang, and she glanced at the screen, sitting upright in her seat before she answered. "Yes?"

That was weird. She didn't usually answer her phone like that. She obviously knew who had called but wasn't excited to talk to them. That or their call made her anxious, which led me to believe it was about Jed.

She was silent as she listened for a few moments, then said, "Okay. Thanks." Then she hung up.

I watched as she placed the phone on her desk, then pretended to go back to work.

"Who was that?"

She forced a laugh. "I thought *I* was the nosy one."

"Was it about Jed?"

She glanced over at me and rolled her eyes. "Don't worry about it, Rose."

I considered pressing her, but I didn't want to force it out of her. I wanted her to tell me because she wanted to. "Okay, but if you change your mind, I'm here and ready to listen."

Releasing a groan, she got to her feet. "I'm gonna get some coffee at the coffee shop. You want me to get you something?"

"Sure."

I gave her a look that made her face soften.

"Don't look at me like that," she said. "It's not personal. I just need to keep this to myself right now."

"Okay," I said. "I trust you."

Something flickered through her eyes, but it passed too quickly to interpret. "Text me your order," she said, rushing for the door, leaving me to wonder what I'd done to send her running. Why would telling her I trusted her upset her? My thoughts went to dark places, but I quickly shut them down. There was no way Jed or Neely Kate would betray me or Joe. There was no denying we'd all been part of the mess, some of us more than others, but so far, our names had been kept out of it. She'd sooner go to prison herself than implicate any of us. So, what did she feel guilty about?

I grabbed my phone and texted her to get my usual drink plus a blueberry muffin. I'd just pushed send when the bells on the door rang. Had Neely Kate changed her mind about telling me what was going on? "I was just sending you—"

My voice cut off when I saw Betsy Simmons walk into the office.

She gave me a tight smile. "Hello, Rose. I wondered if maybe we could maybe grab some coffee and have a chat."

My chest tightened as I pushed my chair a few inches away from my desk. "I don't think that's a good idea."

She took several steps closer to me. "I realize Joe isn't interested in seeing me, and I'm trying to respect his wishes, but Rose..." She stopped in front of my desk. "I have a grandchild I saw for a mere few seconds when I dropped by your house on Saturday. I'd like to get to know her. She's family."

I stood behind my desk. "Because she's blood?"

"Of course," she said as though it was a foolish question.

I nearly snorted, but thankfully pulled it back before it escaped. Little did Betsy Simmons know that her grandchild wasn't really blood. But there was no way I was going to tell her that.

"You need to speak to Joe about that, not me."

"Rose," she said, her voice softening. "Can we just speak, mother to mother?" When I didn't say anything, she took it as an invitation to continue. "I confess that I've made mistakes. Quite a few of them, but what Joe doesn't seem to remember is that his father had a hold over all of us. Me included. There were many things I didn't agree with, but I had no choice in the matter. J.R.'s will ruled all."

I had no doubt about that, but I also knew she hadn't been kind to Joe after his father died. Maeve had gone to see him in El Dorado twice and both times, she'd seen Betsy at her finest, meaning her worst.

"Again," I said, "you'll need to talk to Joe about that."

"Rose," she pleaded with tears in her eyes. "I love my son, and I'd love to get to know you and your daughter too—Hope, is it?"

We hadn't told her Hope's name, but it wouldn't have been hard to find out. Which is why it seemed like she hadn't put much initial effort into investigating her grandchild if she thought she had a grandson.

"Betsy," I said, "I refuse to go behind Joe's back."

"How would you feel if Hope turned her back on you when she's grown? Wouldn't you do anything you could to reconcile, even going to her husband asking for help?"

"Or her wife," I said. "She's too young to know who she'll end up with."

Betsy cringed at that, confirming what I'd suspected. She was still as judgmental as she'd been before. She was merely better at hiding it now. There was no denying that other than her parents, she was alone. But there was also no denying she'd gotten herself there.

"Before Kate's death, there might have been a chance of Joe relenting, but your absence from Kate's memorial service was too much for him. He swore he was done."

She looked away, a tear falling down her cheek. Was it real or part of her performance to convince me to help her?

"I was too distraught," she said. "My doctor gave me too much Xanax, and I slept for two days straight. When I came to, I realized I'd missed it."

I had to wonder if she was being truthful, but it still wasn't enough of an explanation. Besides, I wasn't the one who needed to hear it.

"Betsy, I'm going to need you to leave," I said, motioning to the door. It went against everything in me to be so rude, but to entertain her any longer felt like a betrayal to Joe.

She started to say something when the bells on the front door jangled again. We both turned our attention to the entrance, to see Neely Kate walking in, carrying two cups in a drink carrier and small pastry bag. My heart plummeted as a stunned Neely Kate froze in the doorway.

Betsy's back stiffened as she gave Neely Kate her full attention, not that I was surprised she recognized the visual proof of her husband's infidelity, and with an underaged girl, no less.

It took Neely Kate a few seconds before coming to her senses. "I see we have a visitor," she said, trying to sound cheerful as she walked over to her desk, but I knew she was on guard, not that I blamed her.

Betsy looked as taken aback at the sight of my best friend, and it suddenly occurred to me that had Betsy been watching the office, waiting for Neely Kate to leave before making her attempt to ask me to intervene with Joe.

"Betsy was just leaving," I said stiffly, hoping she got the message.

But Betsy continued to stare at Neely Kate before she took a step forward. "You're Neely Kate, aren't you?"

Neely Kate tensed. "Yes."

"I'm Betsy Simmons, Joe's mother." She took a breath, contrition covering her face. "I only recently learned about your existence, and I'd like to offer you my sincerest apology."

Neely Kate gasped. "Excuse me?"

"I bear no ill will toward you, Neely Kate," she said. "You're an innocent caught in all of this. I hear that you and Joe have a relationship now."

I was shocked to see Neely Kate momentarily speechless, but then again, she'd been preparing to be attacked, not apologized to. I had been prepared for it too. Joe had said his mother hadn't been pleased to learn of her existence.

"You hurt Joe," Neely Kate finally said. "You broke his heart."

"I know," Betsy said, clasping her hands in front of her. "That's why I'm here. To make amends."

"He doesn't want to have anything to do with you."

Betsy cast a look over her shoulder at me, then turned back to my best friend. "I know, and I deserve every bit of recrimination that he has for me. But I'd still like to make up for my past actions and have a relationship with him."

Neely Kate's face softened. "I don't think he's open to that."

"I know," Betsy said, her voice breaking. "Do you think *you* could talk to him? Surely you of all people know what it's like to be parentless. I don't wish that for Joe. We need each other."

That wasn't the right tactic to take with Neely Kate. Her father would have likely had her killed had he known of her existence when she was a kid, and her mother had abandoned her when she was twelve. She didn't want to have anything to do with either one of them. So color me astonished when Neely Kate said, "I can't promise you anything, but I'll talk to him."

I barely held back my gasp of surprise.

Betsy rushed forward and grabbed Neely Kate's hand. "Thank you so much."

"Like I said, I can't promise anything," Neely Kate hedged.

"But trying is something," Betsy said, then she gave me another glance. Her face was neutral, but I was pretty sure I saw a flash of anger in her eyes, which I was positive was a jab at me for not agreeing to try to convince Joe to talk to her.

Betsy shook Neely Kate's hand a few times, then dropped it and reached into her purse. She pulled out a business card and shoved it at Neely Kate. "This is where you or Joe can reach me."

Neely Kate took the card and glanced down at it then back up at Betsy.

Betsy tilted her head, studying Neely Kate for a moment before she said softly, "I can see a bit of Joe in you." Then she gave her another smile and walked out the door.

Neely Kate and I watched her leave, then I turned to her. "Are you really gonna try to convince Joe to talk to her?"

She shrugged. "I don't know. Maybe?" Her eyes pleaded with me. "What if she really has changed? Maybe Joe should give her another chance."

"I don't like it," I said, walking over to her desk and reaching for the coffee marked with my name. "I don't trust her."

"So, you don't want Joe to talk to her?"

"I want Joe to make the decision he feels comfortable with, whether it's talk to her or not. I don't want him to feel *pressured* to talk to her. Besides, she took an entirely different stance on Saturday. She barely claimed any responsibility for any of what happened in his childhood or how she treated him and Kate. I don't believe she's seen the light. She's just changed tactics."

Neely Kate pursed her lips, staring out the windows that overlooked the square. Betsy was already out of sight. "All I know is, if my mother showed up and put this much effort into seeing me, I'd see her in a heartbeat."

While I understood why she felt that way—her mother had literally abandoned her and deeply damaged Neely Kate's psyche—it bothered me that I suspected Neely Kate wouldn't meet with her out of curiosity's sake, but because she still needed her mother to love her. Something I was pretty sure Jenny Lynn Rivers was incapable of.

Part of me was worried that deep down, Joe felt the same way.

What a mess.

Chapter Ten

Neely Kate

On Tuesday night, I told Jed I had an early client meeting the next morning and asked him to take Daisy to daycare. I also warned him I might have to work late. I felt guilty that he didn't give a second thought to saying yes. He trusted me implicitly and I knew I was betraying that trust.

Tell him.

Part of me knew what I was about to do was wrong, but I also knew he'd never agree to let me try. I didn't know why, but despite Carter's insistence otherwise, I was sure Skeeter could do something, even if I had no idea what that something was.

So, I kissed my baby and my husband goodbye, then drove to meet Carter up in Magnolia. I'd insisted on meeting there, because the last thing I needed was someone finding my abandoned car and thinking something had happened to me.

As I drove to the rendezvous spot, I used my voice to text to tell Rose that I was taking a mental health day. I'd considered telling her that Daisy was sick, but since they went to the same daycare, she'd likely see her there. I only hoped she didn't run into Jed.

Carter was waiting for me in the grocery store parking lot,

standing next to his car with a phone pressed to his ear. He seemed in the middle of a tense conversation when I pulled in, but he hung up after I'd parked and started to get out of my car.

"Ms. *Carlisle*," he said with a tight grin.

"Cut the crap, Carter," I said. "I'm nervous enough without you starting things."

He chuckled. "If you're so nervous, then I suggest we call this whole thing off."

"No," I said, harsher than I'd intended.

But he didn't seem bothered by it, grinning ear to ear as he gestured to his car. "Then let's get this party started."

I climbed into the passenger seat, once again feeling like I was betraying Jed as I shut the door, but I wasn't turning back now. I'd always followed the philosophy that it was better to ask forgiveness than permission. Even with my own husband.

Carter was silent for the first few minutes, the silence driving me crazy until he said, "So, what's your game plan?"

"I don't know yet."

His brow shot up. "You're going to all this trouble, and you don't even have a plan?"

"I'll figure it out as I go." While that was true, I *did* have a plan. I just didn't feel like sharing it with Carter. I suspected he wouldn't approve, and I didn't want him to have nearly four hours to try to talk me out of it. Or worse—turn around and drive back to Henryetta.

"How did you get away?" he asked.

I knew what he was asking. "Don't you worry about that."

"Do I have to worry about your muscular husband coming after me once we get home?"

"No. He has no idea I'm with you or what I'm doing. Which is why we met in Magnolia." I narrowed my eyes. "But you knew that already, so what are you really gettin' at?"

He paused for a moment. "Does Rose know what you're doin'?"

I hesitated. "No."

He nodded. "That's probably for the best."

"She's moved on, Carter," I said softly. "Skeeter made his choice a year ago when he drove her away, and she found someone who's actually good for her. Nothin' but heartbreak would have come to her if she'd stayed with Skeeter. The only way they would have worked is if they'd moved away, and then she would have had to give up everything she loved. Her business that she started with her now dead sister. Her niece and nephew. Maeve." I paused. "Me."

Carter gripped the wheel of his car, staring out the windshield. "You don't think Skeeter knew that?"

I drew in a breath. "I know he was trying to protect her."

"Not just from Hardshaw, Neely Kate," he said in exasperation. "He was savin' her from himself too. Especially once he found out she was pregnant. He didn't want a kid saddled with his notoriety. He'd had a small taste of it with his own father, and his father was small potatoes compared to Skeeter."

I gaped at him. "Skeeter told you that?"

He snorted. "He didn't have to. I know the man well enough to read between the lines."

"So, he martyred himself for Rose and Hope?"

He snorted even harder. "Skeeter Malcolm's no martyr. He always has a reason for what he does."

"You're suggesting he purposely let himself renege on his deal with the government? That Kate didn't put a kink in his plans?"

"Did he foresee Kate kidnapping Rose and her baby? No. But he was prepared for it if the plan with the alphabet agencies didn't pan out."

"Then what was his plan?" I asked.

He shook his head and said bitterly, "Wouldn't *I* like to know."

"He hasn't told you?"

"Nope."

I stared at him in shock. "But you're his attorney."

"He says to trust him, so that's all I can do, because as much as I've tried to persuade him otherwise, he's not confiding in me."

We were silent for a bit while Carter drove, but he stopped in Little Rock to get more coffee, something I wasn't going to turn down. After that, I asked him questions about being a defense attorney in Fenton County, and he told me about some of his more amusing cases. Turns out that most criminals are stupid.

"Don't you feel guilty getting people who've broken the law out of prison?" I asked.

He turned and gave me a snide look. "I've kept your husband out of prison a time or two, so maybe rethink that holier-than-thou position."

He had a point.

SKEETER WAS BEING HELD in a federal prison in Forrest City, Arkansas, which was close to the Tennessee border. We arrived in town slightly after noon, and Carter suggested we stop and grab lunch before going to the prison, but I told him if I tried to eat, I'd likely vomit.

I hadn't seen Skeeter since we'd all had our big showdown with Kate, and I wasn't sure how he'd react to seeing me. Because, in the end, in her delusion, Kate had kidnapped Hope hoping to lure Rose to her death. Kate knew how devastated I was over my infertility and had worked out her weird plan to get me a baby. And since she saw Rose as competition for my affection, her plan took care of two problems at the same time.

Nevertheless, her plan hadn't made sense, not that Kate was thinking sensibly at the end. If Rose had died, Hope would have gone to her father—Joe. But part of me would always wonder if somehow Kate had known the truth. And if she *had* known, I hoped to God she hadn't told anyone else before she'd been killed.

Saving Hope and Rose had been the reason Skeeter was in prison, and the ultimate reason for it was because of me, even if I hadn't been privy to or approved of Kate's plan. But I couldn't help wondering if Skeeter blamed me. Was that blame, along with Jed's perceived betrayal, one of the reasons Jed was going to be questioned? Had Skeeter set it up to make us pay? If so, I was here to see if I could find a way to atone for our sins.

The dark clouds in the sky were heavy with rain, casting a gloomy mood as we walked across the parking lot to the entrance to the prison. I'd visited Witt a few times when he'd been incarcerated, so I was familiar with all the heavy security, but it didn't make me any less anxious.

"Oh, by the way," Carter said when we were several feet from the entrance. "You're my assistant."

I laughed. "How many assistants have you brought here?"

"You're the first."

He opened the door before I could question him. He told the guards he was James Malcolm's attorney and that I was his assistant, and that he needed to speak to Skeeter about his case. The guard looked me up and down and I was sure he was going to tell me I wouldn't be allowed in, but then Carter reached out his hand to shake with the guard, and I was pretty sure I saw a folded hundred-dollar bill in the guard's hand when he pulled it away.

I hadn't been prepared for that, but this wasn't the first instance of Carter bribing law enforcement and people in authority. I knew he'd paid off some of the staff at the hospital when Kate had been incarcerated in a psych ward. I also knew Skeeter'd had a source in the Fenton County sheriff's department, and I suspected he had contacts in other places of authority too.

So, why was he in prison? Were the FBI, DEA, and ATF outside of his sphere of influence? Maybe, but I couldn't help thinking that being here was part of his plan. I just had no idea what that plan could be. Apparently—if Carter was telling the truth—neither did he. His frustration seemed too genuine to be faking it.

The guards patted us down and we checked in our phones and other personal effects, leaving Carter with a notepad and a pen before they led us down multiple dingy halls. The guard stopped outside a solid metal door, unlocked it, then pushed it open.

"Wait in here while they get him," the guard said, then practically shoved us in before closing the door.

The room was small—about ten-foot square—with a narrow window high up on the wall that let in a sliver of natural light. Fluorescent lights hung from the ten-foot ceilings. A wooden table sat in the middle of the room, with a metal bar down the center of the table, presumably for handcuffs. Two metal chairs were on our side of the table and a single metal chair sat on the other. A door was in the middle of the wall opposite us. It was a depressing space with dingy gray walls, but then again, we *were* in a prison.

Carter gestured for me to sit, and I did because if I didn't, I'd start to pace. I knew I needed to appear confident, but right now I was scared to death. I wasn't sure what I was hoping for was even possible, and yet, I was pinning our entire future on it.

Carter sat beside me and put a hand lightly on my upper arm. "Hey," he said, then waited for me to lift my gaze to his. "Just be yourself. He knows you, so don't pretend to be anything else. Just plead your case."

I nodded, feeling close to breaking down, so I took a deep breath and tried to settle my nerves. I needed to be myself, but I couldn't fall apart, either. Skeeter Malcolm abhorred weakness.

Several minutes later, the door across the room opened and Skeeter, wearing a bright orange jumpsuit, appeared in the doorway. His gaze landed on Carter then quickly shifted to me. A momentary look of surprise filled his eyes before it shifted to indifference. A guard stood behind him and he shut the door after Skeeter entered the room.

Skeeter moved over to the table and pulled out the chair, the metal scraping against the concrete floor. When he took his seat, he leaned back and looked me up and down.

"When I heard Hale had a friend with him, I can't say I expected it to be you."

I wasn't sure if that was a good thing or a bad one.

"How're you doin', Skeeter?" I asked, then immediately regretted it.

He held his hands out at his sides. "Oh, you know…" He glanced around the room.

"Sorry. Stupid question."

"So, to what do I owe this visit?" he asked, but he seemed tense, casting a sidelong glance at Carter before returning it back to me.

I felt like an idiot for not realizing he'd jump to conclusions seeing me here. "This isn't about Rose," I said softly. "She's okay."

He gave a slight nod, then seemed to relax a little. "Then what are you doin' here, because I can't imagine you came all this way to shoot the shit."

I swallowed hard, suddenly unsure about my plan, but Carter beat me to action.

"I told her the FBI was planning to interview Jed after the first of the year."

Skeeter didn't move or say anything, which made me more nervous.

"First," I said, my voice breaking. I took a breath then started again. "First, I'm not sure I ever thanked you properly for all you did to help me find Ronnie."

"Well, now," he said, crossing his leg over his knee and resting his hands on top of his raised knee. "I didn't exactly find him now, did I? Your crazy-ass sister did."

It was true. While Skeeter and Carter had hired private investigators to search for my wayward husband so I could serve divorce papers, it was Kate who had found him and offered him to me as a gift.

"Still," I said, "you and Carter went to a lot of effort to find him. I didn't have the resources you did."

"It wasn't an entirely selfless motive," Skeeter said. "I wanted to find him too, so don't go canonizin' me. Not for that."

"I knew the whole time you wanted to find him too," I said with a huff. "I'm not *entirely* stupid, so I'm grateful that you shared what you did with me. You could have kept all your information to yourself and told me to get lost."

He barely nodded in acknowledgment. I'd known he wasn't looking for Ronnie to just help me, but it wasn't entirely selfish either. I was sure he'd also done it for Rose since I was her best friend. And likely for Jed, since Skeeter had to know he'd liked me. That was one of the reasons it was so shocking when Skeeter had turned his back on Jed for wanting to be with me.

"No matter the reasons," I said, "I'm still grateful." I shot a quick glance to Carter. "To both of you."

Carter gave me a tight smile.

"So, while you already did me a favor which I haven't repaid," I said, "I'm here asking for another."

Skeeter released a little chuckle. "In case the orange suit and the maximum security to get into the place didn't clue you in, I'm in prison. I don't know how helpful I'll be in here." His leg dropped to the floor, and he leaned forward. "I presume this has to do with Jed."

I nodded, then swallowed again. I really should have drunk some water before I came in. "Yes. Carter was kind enough to warn me that it was likely to happen and told me to get Jed an attorney."

Skeeter grinned, but it didn't reach his eyes. "Then I still don't know why you're here, seeing how I'm not an attorney."

I rolled my eyes, starting to feel more like myself. "No kiddin'? I want to know why *you* think they're wantin' to talk to him."

"Hell if I know," he said, sitting back again. "Could be they want to dig into our *alleged* criminal activities in Fenton County and they want to put him away too. Seems like a county sheriff's job to me, but then again, we *did* deal with some underground arms trading—allegedly, of course—so maybe they caught wind of that? Then again, that would be the ATF, unless the FBI wrestled it away from 'em."

"Do you think they're lookin' for information about *you*?"

He remained silent.

I took that as encouragement to continue. "Last I heard, you're here on some ridiculous charges that don't amount to a hill of beans, yet they won't let you post bail. Which tells me they're still workin' on what to charge you with, *or—*" I made sure I had his attention "—they're pressuring you to give them something. Seeing as how you're still here, if that's the case, you apparently haven't given it to them, so now they're goin' after people you care about."

"Care about," he scoffed. "Jed and I parted ways. I don't give a shit about what he does or what happens to him."

"You're many things, Skeeter Malcolm," I snapped, "but I never took you for a flat-out liar."

His gaze darkened and the hair on the back of my neck stood on end. He wasn't restrained in any way and could easily reach across the table and grab my throat, but I knew he never would. It would kill Rose if she found out he hurt me, but more importantly, never in all the time I'd known him had I felt threatened by him. Sure, he had a scary reputation—and with just cause—but I knew he'd never hurt me, at least not physically.

He looked away but didn't say a word.

"Have they asked you about your relationship with Jed?" I asked.

"They've asked me all sorts of things," he grumbled, still not looking at me.

"Are they goin' after Jed to find out what y'all did in the county or to see if he was involved with your agreement with Hardshaw?"

He shook his head, his focus on the wall. "Hell if I know. Maybe both."

"Why not rat him out?" I asked, my heart pounding against my rib cage, terrified to hear the answer. "You could probably work out some kind of deal if you gave them info on him."

He released a bitter laugh. "They're not after him. He's small potatoes. They're after bigger things."

"Like what?"

He turned to look at me, his eyes ice cold. "It's none of your damn business."

My back stiffened. "It is if it involves my husband."

"Then why isn't *he* here?" he snapped. "Why send his wife?"

"Because he doesn't know I'm here!" I shouted. "He doesn't know about any of this!"

He sat back in his chair, his eyes widening. "You don't say." He shifted his gaze to Carter.

"I thought it best to tell Neely Kate first," Carter said.

Skeeter stared at Carter for a long moment, but to his credit, Carter didn't so much as flinch, just waited him out.

When he realized he wasn't going to get a reaction, Skeeter turned to me, looking exasperated. "What is it you want from *me*?"

"I want you to get them to back off Jed."

He laughed again, this time sounding more amused. "Don't you think if I had that kind of power, I'd get *myself* out of here?"

"That's just it," I said. "I think you *do* have the power." I decided to play the ace up my sleeve, prepared to face his wrath. "Skeeter—if they're goin' after people you care about, will they go after Rose next?"

He slammed his hand on the table so hard I flinched. His eyes blazed with anger, his jaw clenched so hard veins popped out on his forehead. "You leave her out of this!"

"I *want* to leave her out of this," I said insistently. "Jed did his share of bad things, so ultimately, if push comes to shove, he'll need to answer for them. But we both know Rose did everything she did to help others. Joe. Mason. *You*."

Skeeter didn't look any less angry, but I pushed on, figuring I had nothing to lose.

"What is it they want from you, Skeeter? Because I can't help thinking if they were after Jed, they would have come askin' questions months ago."

He shook his head, his face still flushed.

"I'm scared for Rose," I said, my voice breaking.

His fist clenched on the table.

"She's already been through so much, and she's finally happy. She doesn't deserve to be dragged back into all of this."

He pushed out a ragged sigh and a war seemed to wage on his face before he asked, "How is she?"

I'd just told him she was happy, so I knew he was looking for details. I was happy to oblige. "The landscape business is doin' well, and so is the nursery. We've got so many new clients we can hardly keep up with designs. Maeve and Anna are running the nursery and doin' a good job. Violet gave me partial ownership until Ashley and Mikey are old enough to take over, but Maeve's got it under control, so I work mostly with Rose." Then I added, "And all of my profit from the nursery either goes back into the business or into a bank account for when the kids are older."

He didn't look surprised, but the only person I'd told about the bank account was Jed. Even Rose didn't know, because I knew she'd insist I keep part of the profits. But Jed and I had enough money, and we'd both agreed we wanted Violet's kids to have it.

There was a hungry look in Skeeter's eyes, and now that I'd

given him a taste of Rose's life, he was starving for more. I had no doubts that Carter kept him informed as best he could about her life, but I was her best friend. Other than Joe, I knew more about her than anyone else.

"She loves bein' a mother," I said softly, "and she's darn good at it."

"I wouldn't expect anything less," he said with the hint of a smile.

"She works part time and tries to do some of her work at home so she can be with Hope and Ashley and Mikey, but once she's there, she usually wants to be with them. She tried bringin' Hope to the office, which worked when she was an infant, but when she got more mobile it was hard, so she's in a daycare now."

I saw the way his eyes lit up when I mentioned Hope, so I said, "Hope's the spittin' image of Rose. Dark hair, sweet, and smart as a whip, but a tiny bit ornery too. She must have a little of her dad in her because she head butted Santa a week ago and broke his nose. Apparently, it caused quite a scene."

I wondered if I'd gone too far mentioning that, but I could have been talking about Joe. The pleased look in his eyes told me he knew I wasn't.

"Joe's good to her," I said quietly. "He's a good daddy too—to both Hope and Violet's kids. He doesn't take any of them for granted and he more than pulls his weight with housework and childcare."

"I never would have done any of that shit," he said in a low growl.

"I know," I said. And I knew Rose did too, but I wasn't about to say so.

"You said the business is doin' well," he said, staring at the wall again. "She doin' okay with money?"

"She and Joe aren't rich, by any means, but they're doin' okay."

He nodded. "Everything else goin' okay? She runnin' into any problems with Mike and the kids?"

"Actually…"

He turned to look at me. His eyes were cold as ice, but I knew it wasn't directed at me.

"Mike's case still hasn't gone to trial, and Rose is having to split custody with his parents. They're being buttheads about the whole thing and makin' everyone's lives miserable, especially the kids. I think his parents see 'em as a trophy to show off to their friends, instead of wanting to be with them. Mikey was sick this weekend and his grandparents still made him go to church. Plus, they're just not good with kids. They won't let them make any noise or a mess. They're just too militaristic. They're the kind of people who are better having their grandkids for a few hours at a time, not days at a time. The whole thing has Rose pretty upset."

"So why doesn't Rose have custody?"

"Mike has to either sign it over to Rose or they have to wait until he's convicted and then work it out, although a mediator told Rose they'll likely keep the same arrangement."

He tapped the table once with his index finger. "So, the ideal arrangement would be for Rose to have full custody and see Mike's parents less often."

"In a perfect world, yes. It's what Violet wanted."

The mention of Violet's name seemed to stir something in him. He fisted his hand then said, "I'll take care of it."

I stared at him in disbelief. "What do you mean you'll take care of it?"

He looked into my eyes with a glare that brooked no argument. "Exactly what I said: I'll take care of it."

He tapped his finger again, glancing over at Carter for several seconds before turning back to me. He no longer looked angry, but he didn't look jovial. "I'll take care of the Jed situation too."

"What?" Carter cried out, nearly jumping off his seat.

"How?" I asked at the same time.

"You don't need to worry about the how," Skeeter said, ignoring Carter. "But I'm asking for something in return."

I wasn't exactly surprised, but I was a little disappointed. I'd hoped he'd do it because Jed had been his friend since childhood, not to use his friend's freedom as a bargaining tool. "What?"

He cocked a brow. "You're askin' what? You're not just agreein'?"

"I'm not foolish enough to agree to just anything," I sassed back. "I've heard the story about Rumpelstiltskin."

He gave me a questioning look, then turned to Carter.

"Just go with it," Carter said with a grin.

Skeeter gave me a hard stare. "What I'm about to ask stays between you, me, and Carter. You can't tell Jed, and you definitely can't tell Rose or Joe. If you do, the whole deal's off."

"I'm listening…" I said hesitantly. I wasn't sure I could agree to keeping a secret from the people closest to me, but I was willing to hear him out.

"I'll make Jed's questioning go away, but in return, you'll send a report with photos once a month."

I gave him a leery glance. "What kind of report?"

"About Rose." He paused. "And the baby. It has to be handwritten—no computer printout to leave a trace. It needs to be at least one page long, preferably more, with details about their lives." His eyes narrowed. "And I'll expect updates about the situation regarding her niece and nephew."

Was I betraying Rose if I agreed to such a thing? It felt like I was, but at the same time, I understood why he was asking. He could ask Rose for the details, and she'd gladly give them, but he wouldn't do that to her. He wanted her to be free. But I didn't mind being tied to him by this thin chain. Not if it guaranteed that Jed—and likely Rose—would be safe.

"Okay," I said softly. "I'll be happy to do it. Do we have a deal?"

He stuck out his hand and when I reached mine out to his, he engulfed it in a strong, but not crushing shake.

When I pulled my hand away, I said, "I would have given you

the letter for nothin', you know. I know what you gave up to protect 'em. And not just from Kate."

"Water under the bridge," he grunted, then got to his feet.

I stood too. "Thank you, Skeeter."

"Don't be thankin' me," he said gruffly. "It's a business deal, no more, no less."

I nodded, because I had more mushy things to say, but I knew he wasn't interested in hearing them.

"The letters will go to Carter," he said. "Never, *under any circumstances*, will you send them to me or attach my name to them."

I was caught by surprise, but it quickly faded. He was still protecting them. "Yeah, okay."

He nodded, then moved to the door on his side and pounded. The door opened almost immediately, revealing the guard who'd been there before. I supposed he'd been there waiting.

Skeeter started to walk out, then stopped and turned his head halfway so I could only see his profile. "For what it's worth," he said, his voice thick with emotion, "I knew you were right for him the first time I saw you givin' him hell."

Then he walked out the door and it closed behind him.

And that's when I knew Skeeter's betrayal hadn't been a betrayal at all.

He'd pushed Jed away to save him.

Chapter Eleven

Joe

I didn't want to be here.

I'd left Bruce Wayne with some lighting jobs, and my wife and kids would soon be waiting for me in our cozy farmhouse. The last place I wanted to be was in El Dorado, meeting my mother at a coffee shop.

But here I was.

Neely Kate had called me a few days ago and told me that my mother had dropped in at the landscape office to try to coerce me to talk to her. Funnily enough, while Rose had mentioned it, she never put any pressure on me to meet with her. It was Neely Kate who convinced me I'd likely regret it if I didn't.

"I can come with you," she'd said. "I know you want to protect Rose from her, but that woman has no power over me. Not anymore."

I wanted to ask her what the *not anymore* meant, but I was too dead set on defending the reason for my refusal. "You of all people should understand why I don't want to see her."

"Do I think she's changed?" Neely Kate asked. "Not a chance, but years from now, you'll wonder. So, give her one last chance—let her know it's her last chance—then let her show her true colors and be done with her. And then you'll truly be free of her."

She was right, and I told her so. She gloated just as much as I'd expected, and I still marveled that we were this close after knowing we were siblings for less than a year.

I'd told Rose about our conversation, and she'd said she agreed with her best friend, but it was ultimately my decision, no one else's, and she'd respect whatever I decided.

I called my mother and suggested we meet for coffee so we could "chat." She suggested she could come to the farmhouse or somewhere in Henryetta, but I didn't want her anywhere near where I lived, so I said I'd come to El Dorado. I figured there would be people around who might know her and fear for her reputation would keep her from causing a scene. Only, as I sat at the table waiting for her to show up, I wondered if I'd screwed up. If I wanted her true colors to come out, I should have picked a place where no one knew her.

Too late now.

She walked in a few minutes late, stopping in the doorway to scan the small dining area. Her eyes landed on me and a warm smile lit up her face. My heart gave a little sputter, remembering how hard I tried to get her to give me that smile when I was growing up. And how infrequently my mother gave it to Kate. I reminded myself that it wasn't real. That smile was just another weapon in her arsenal for getting what she wanted.

She walked over to the table and glanced down, smiling even more when she saw the teapot and cup on the table in front of the empty chair. "You got me tea." The pride in her voice was unmistakable.

"Don't read too much into it," I said, catching her gaze and holding it. I almost told her that I'd gotten her a drink so I wouldn't have to wait for her to order and prolong this meeting any longer than it needed to be. But that seemed too antagonistic. I needed to play this neutral for now.

She sat, and I took in her light gray wool pants and her light blue silk blouse as she shrugged off her navy-blue wool coat. She still dressed well, so she'd found money somewhere.

I picked up my mug of coffee and waited for her to begin.

She gave me an uncomfortable look, like she'd expected me to say more, but then she picked up the teapot and poured some into her cup. "Thank you for meeting me. I would have come to you to keep it easier for you. I'm sure it was difficult to get away from your work and your family to come all this way."

"I decided to make it easier for you," I said. It was partially a lie, but it *was* closer to her parents.

She gave me a questioning look, then her brows shot up— well, barely shot up. I'd already suspected her forehead was full of Botox. "Oh! You think I was living in El Dorado." She shook her head as she poured honey into her cup and began to stir. "No, I'm living in Little Rock now."

I stared at her in surprise. "Grandma and Grandpa moved to Little Rock?"

"Oh, no," she said with a small laugh as she continued to stir her tea. The spoon made a gentle tinging sound as it hit the side of the cup. "I wasn't there long. I have a job up in Little Rock." Her face lit up. "Can you believe it?"

"A job?" I asked, nearly choking on the sip of coffee I'd just taken. "Doing what?" I grimaced. "Sorry, that came out more aggressively than I intended."

She laughed. "I'm sure it came as a shock. I swore I'd never have a job doing anything other than mothering my children, running our house, and charity work, but desperate times…" She let her voice trail off as she picked up her teacup and took a sip.

I had to admit I was curious, so I asked, "What are you doing?"

"I work for an interior decorator. She heard I was having a bit of a sticky financial mess and offered me a job. She'd seen all the spreads done in the magazines about our house and told me I had excellent taste. She said many of her clients show her the photos and say they want exactly what we had, so why not hire the source of the design to help her?"

I took another sip of my coffee then said, "I'm sure you're good at it." I meant it. While she'd hired decorators, she'd done most of the work herself. They'd merely made the purchases with their sources and discounts.

My mother beamed. "Thank you."

I set down my mug and rested my forearms on the table. "I have to admit I'm curious as to why you reached out to me now."

She made a face, still clutching her teacup. "Several factors, really. I regret the way I treated you after your father's untimely demise."

I nearly called her out on her phrasing, especially since I'd been the one who killed him, but let it go to keep the conversation going.

"And moving on from the life I had with your father… I realized how toxic our family had become." She set her cup down then reached over and placed her hand on mine. "I'm so proud of how you're choosing to raise your family, and how involved you are in your daughter's life. You'll be an amazing father, Joe, and if nothing else comes from this conversation, I at least wanted you to know that."

"Thank you," I said past the lump in my throat. I'd never, ever, expected her to tell me anything like that. In fact, I'd been prepared to hear the opposite.

Her head tilted to the side, and she gave me a soft smile. "I can see by the look on your face that's not what you expected to hear."

"No."

Her smiled tightened, then she removed her hand from mine and picked up her cup. "I met your sister, you know."

It took me a second to realize she was talking about Neely Kate. "I heard."

"She's a *lovely* girl. I told her I didn't hold her parentage against her." She took another sip of her tea. "In fact, I'm glad you have her. Especially after all the grief Kate caused you and the family, especially to your wife and child."

She was catching me off guard again, but before I let myself bask in the new form my mother had taken, something deep down reminded me that in the past, this was often how she lured in her victims. Catch them off guard with unexpected compliments and lavish praise, before getting them to give her what she wanted. She was like a cobra, hypnotizing her prey, then once they were relaxed and complacent, she went in for the strike. And half the time, the poor fools didn't even know they'd been had.

My mother was doing the exact same thing to me now.

My back stiffened, but she didn't seem to notice my shift.

"Besides," she continued, taking a sip of her tea before she gave me a pleading look. "It's Christmas, which means it's time for family. I want to be with my *family*, Joe."

"Funny how Christmas was all about showing off to your friends and neighbors with your extravagant Christmas Eve parties. Kate and I were afterthoughts."

Her face made a delicate grimace that anyone else would have taken for embarrassment, but I knew better.

"I suppose it appeared that way," she said. "But I was just as much a victim of your father as you and your sister were."

That gave me pause, because I knew there was some truth to that statement. The question was, how much? Kids never saw their parents the way they really were. They were either too self-involved or their parents hid it from them. With my family, it was probably a little of both.

"Yes," I conceded. "You were a victim too."

A small look of triumph filled her eyes but then it was gone.

"What do you want, exactly?" I asked. "Did you show up at my door because you want to spend Christmas with us? Stay in the spare bedroom so you can be there to watch the kids open gifts on Christmas morning?"

"Kids?" she asked, then her eyes lit up. "Is Rose pregnant again?"

"What? No." I shook my head. "Her niece and nephew live with us part time. Rose's sister died a year ago and their father … isn't available."

"Oh." She looked disappointed. "I was hoping a Joseph Simmons the third was on the way."

I gritted my teeth. "No child of mine will ever be named Joseph the third."

She patted my hand. "Of course not. We wouldn't want the poor baby to be saddled with your father's scandalous reputation." She retracted her hand then asked stiffly, "When will Rose's niece and nephew's father return?"

"Not for some time."

She cocked her head. "Which means you're stuck raising children that aren't your own?"

I set the mug down harder than I'd intended. If only she knew the truth about Hope—but she never would. I'd make damn sure of it. "It's a *blessing* to have Ashley and Mikey in our home. We love them, and we're tryin' to get full custody."

She gasped. "Do you really want to saddle yourself with such a responsibility?"

I let out a sharp laugh that drew attention from the two young mothers with babies at a table next to us. "I love those kids. Insult them again and this meeting will be over without so much as a goodbye."

She bit her bottom lip then leaned closer. "I'm sorry. I can see that you care about them. I just don't want you to feel trapped. Rose has such a good heart, I can see how she might take in her dead sister's children and not give you a choice in the matter. And you have such a good heart, you'd go along with it whether you wanted to or not."

I drew in a breath to restrain my anger. "How would you know if Rose has a good heart? You don't know the first thing about her. You and Dad never gave her a chance. You decided she wasn't good enough for me and dismissed her." I narrowed my eyes. "I believe you might have called her Fenton County Trash."

She had the good sense to look genuinely embarrassed. "I regret saying those awful things, but your father—"

I shook my head. "No. I don't want to hear it. You meant every word. You both were worried about my political campaign."

"Joe…" She started to reach for me again, then stopped. "Joe. I was a fool. I'll admit that I wanted certain things for you—certain people—and even though you protested, I thought we knew better. We were wrong." She paused. "*I* was wrong. I'm sorry. Truly I am. I would love to make it up to you both."

My curiosity got the better of me. "How?"

Her face went blank. "Excuse me?"

"How do you plan to make it up to us?"

"Well … I …"

I snorted. "Yeah, I figured." Sitting back in my chair, I held her gaze. "I'm still not sure why I'm here. You said you want to spend Christmas with us. What does that entail?"

She took a moment then clasped her hands on the table. "I've met someone."

I suspected I knew what she was hinting at, but I wasn't going to make it easy on her. "You mean you've made friends with your new coworkers?"

"Well, it *was* through my new job," she said with a coy look. "His name is Marvin and he's an investment banker. He bought a new house after his wife died and he needed help decorating it."

"You want Marvin to come to our house for Christmas too?" I asked in confusion.

"No…" She took a breath. "I'd love for you and your family to come for dinner on Christmas Day. You can meet Marvin's children too."

"Why?" I blurted out.

"What?" she asked in confusion.

"Why would I want to meet Marvin's children?"

"Joe," she said with gentle exasperation. "Because if things continue the way they are, they'll be your new siblings." When I didn't say anything, she continued, "Marvin wants to meet you and your family. I thought it would be nice for everyone to get acquainted on Christmas."

"We could meet next weekend. Why Christmas?"

"Well … Marvin's very busy, and Christmas is the only day all of his children will be available." When I didn't say anything, she added, "Besides, Marvin would love to talk to you about your future."

"Why would a man I've never met be interested in my future?"

"Because he knows you're important to me," she said with mild exasperation. "And he knows how hard it is to raise a family on blue collar wages. If you're raising three children, it's even harder."

"How altruistic of him," I said with a hint of sarcasm. "And does Marvin have a solution for my situation?"

"He does!" she said brightly. "I've told him how clever you are and that you're college educated. And he says your experience with the state police will be an asset."

I shook my head. "An asset for *what?*"

"A job, silly. There's to be an opening at his branch, and he wants to offer it to *you.*"

I was surprised by this turn of events. She'd ignored me for nearly two years. Why was she concerned about my profession and my family's well-being *now?* "I have a job, Mother."

"You *had* a job," she said stiffly. "You used to be a high-ranking sheriff's official, and now you dabble in the dirt for your wife's cute little business. You're a Simmons, Joseph. Ambition is part of your DNA. You need a *career.* Don't you want *more?*"

"I'm perfectly content," I snapped. "I *love* my life, and if you'd spent even half a minute asking me if I was happy, you'd know that. Do I want to work with my wife forever? I don't know. But I don't have to decide right now. For now, I can just love my family and be content, something you and Dad *never* were." I stood and grabbed my coat off the back of my chair. "No, I won't be coming for Christmas dinner, and I sure as hell don't want a job at a bank. That sounds like a nightmare." I leaned forward. "Which only confirms you never knew me at all."

I turned around and headed for the door, with my mother calling out my name. I didn't stop, just kept walking until I reached my car.

"Joe!" my mother called out behind me from the sidewalk. It was the pain and desperation in her voice that stopped me.

I turned to look at her, my hand on the door handle, and waited.

She had her coat slung over her shoulder and her purse in her hand, but her eyes were wide with fear. Did she really want to connect with me, and she was terrified she'd blown it? I'd had money my entire life until I'd turned my back on my parents. She probably thought I wanted it again. Had this been her sick and twisted way of making amends?

The tightness in my chest loosened.

"Joe, I'm just going to lay it out and tell you the truth."

I dropped my hand from the door handle. "I guess there's a first time for everything."

"I suppose I deserve that." She took a step toward me. "It's important to Marvin that you're there. He's big into family and he doesn't understand why we don't see each other more."

"Have you considered continuing your little truth journey and telling him the real reason?"

She cringed. "I've admitted that I've not been the best mother, but I want to *try*, Joe. I want a fresh start with you."

I almost fell for it. Almost. But she hadn't reached out to me until Marvin was in her life, asking questions. If family was important to her new boyfriend, he likely wouldn't want to continue seeing a woman who was estranged from her only son.

"You want to try because of Marvin, not because you want a relationship with me or Hope." I shook my head. "We won't be coming to dinner, and as far as I'm concerned, this is the last time we'll be speaking."

"Joseph!" she shouted in dismay. "You don't mean that!"

"I totally mean it," I said, more calmly than I felt. "I don't want you anywhere near my kids. They don't need to be exposed to your poisonous manipulation." I jerked the car door open. "This is goodbye, Mom. I hope you get the life you deserve."

Then I drove away and never looked back.

Chapter Twelve

Rose

Joe had texted me that he was done with his meeting with his mother and would be home in about an hour. I was worried that he hadn't told me how it had gone, but I didn't press. It would be better to hear what happened face to face.

I got Ashley started on her homework and got a pot of chili going, then took Mikey out in the front yard to play catch with Muffy. I sat in a chair on the porch with Hope on my lap, while she babbled and chewed on her teething toy. Hopefully, her stubborn tooth would come in soon.

I'd been worried about Neely Kate for most of the day. She'd taken the day off, saying she needed a mental health day. I knew she was worried about Jed, and it had to be eating at her, but last I'd heard, she hadn't told Jed, and she hadn't contacted Mason. Avoidance wasn't her usual way of handling things, so her behavior had me even more worried. But I did the only thing I could by telling her to do what she needed to do, and that I was there for her.

So, I was pretty shocked when she called me in the middle of the afternoon, telling me that the whole Jed situation had been a false alarm. That Carter said he'd been wrong about the FBI wanting to talk to Jed, and everything was fine.

It was a Christmas miracle.

I was relieved for both of them, but I wondered how Carter had gotten it so wrong. I didn't know Carter Hale as well as Neely Kate did, but making a mistake like that seemed totally out of character for him.

Then, right before Joe got home, my cell phone rang, and I saw Fenton County Jail on the caller ID. The only calls we got from the jail were from Mike when he wanted to talk to the kids. I considered telling Mikey to come inside, but this call felt off. Mike never called them late in the afternoon. He always called them on Sunday evening.

I answered the call and accepted the charges as I stood and moved to the far end of the porch. I doubted Mikey would pay any attention to my call, but I wanted to be safe. Thankfully, Hope seemed content with me holding her while she watched Muffy run around, chasing Mikey's ball.

"Hello?" I said once the call made the connection. "Mike?"

"Rose," he said, his voice gruff. "Is Joe there?"

"No," I said, fear racing through my blood. "He won't be home for a bit. Why?"

"That's okay," he said, his voice sounding shaky. "You're the one I needed to talk to. You can tell Joe when you get a chance."

"Okay…" I was starting to feel sick. "Is everything okay?"

He was silent for a long moment. "I'm gonna take the plea deal, which means I'll be in prison for a while."

"Oh, Mike," I said, my voice breaking. "The kids will be devastated."

"Nah," he said. "They'll be okay, but I have a big ask of you. And Joe too."

"Anything."

"I want you and Joe to have full custody of the kids. No more splittin' time with my parents. My parents can see them one weekend a month, but only if it works with the kids' schedules and only if they want to. I trust you to be fair with that decision." He released a ragged breath. "I hear the kids aren't really enjoying their visits with my parents, and I heard Mikey was real sick this weekend, but they took him to church anyway."

How had he known that? Had his parents told him?

"They used to pull that shit with me when I was a kid," he continued, "and we both know Mikey needed to be tucked under the covers watching cartoons, not forced to sit in a boring church service. So, they need to be with you—and Joe."

I couldn't believe what he was saying. "Mike."

"I know you'll raise them as your own, and Joe will too. This is for the best for everyone. Especially my kids." He let out a sob. "This is what Violet wanted anyway."

"Mike, I swear to you I will love them with everything in me," I said through my tears.

"I know you will," he said, then sniffed. "Just don't let them forget me, okay?"

"Never, I promise," I insisted. "You're their father, and I'll make sure they not only remember it, but also know how much you love them. Plus, we'll bring them to see you."

"I doubt I'll be here in the county jail much longer," he said. "It's bound to be a longer drive."

"We'll make it work."

We were both silent for several long seconds before Mike said, "I'm really sorry I turned into such a dick. I tried to keep Violet and the kids away from you, and I deeply regret it." He paused. "I regret a lot of things."

"We all have regrets," I said.

"Some of us more than others."

Little did he know I had a mountain of them.

"I'll have my attorney draw up a custody agreement," he said, then released another soft sob. "I'll leave it up to your discretion when they see my parents at Christmas."

"I won't keep them from their grandparents," I assured him. "They need that connection to you."

"See?" he said with a soft laugh. "I knew you'd be fair." Then he hung up without saying goodbye.

Chapter Thirteen

James

I wasn't surprised when Carter came back to the prison the next day, nor was I surprised that he knew what I'd been up to since he'd left.

"I heard Mike Beauregard accepted a plea deal," he said before I even had a chance to sit down.

"Is that so?" I said good-naturedly. "I suppose that's a good thing, isn't it?"

He didn't look amused. "I know you had something to do with it."

"Phone calls may have been made," I said cryptically.

"What did you promise?"

I sat back in my chair. "Who says I promised anything?"

"Skeeter…" he practically growled.

"Beauregard's a father, and what do most fathers want?"

A deep scowl settled on his face. "Your father and mine wanted their next bottle of booze. Somehow, I don't think you promised him that."

"Most *normal* fathers."

"Wouldn't know," he snapped. "Never met one."

I snorted. "They want to make sure their kids are protected."

Something flashed in his eyes, but he didn't respond.

"I assured him that his kids would have trusts waiting for them after they graduate from high school, so college won't be an issue." I wrinkled my forehead. "We both know Rose won't be able to put three kids through a good college with her business. It's successful, but Fenton County's not big enough to provide for all of that."

"So, you need me to set up two individual trusts like the one you set up for Hope?" he said, pulling out a legal pad and pen from his bag.

Hearing my daughter's name sent a sharp bolt of pain through my chest. I'd never, ever wanted a kid, and I never wanted Rose to go through with her pregnancy, but now that our daughter was born, I'd move heaven and earth to make sure she was safe and taken care of. "Set 'em up with fifty K for now. We'll discuss how much more to add later."

"Sure," he said, writing it down.

"You could have given me a heads-up about Neely Kate showin' up," I grunted.

"And have you refuse to see us? Yeah, I don't think so." He glanced up. "Let me go on the record stating that I don't think it was fair to promise her that the Feds would back off Jed. You don't have that kind of power. I had to bite my tongue all the way back to Fenton County. I suggested it wouldn't be a bad idea to seek out an attorney anyway, but she has total faith that you're handling it."

I shrugged. Carter didn't know about my secret meetings with a couple of agents from the FBI, and for now, I intended to keep it that way. It had been one of those meetings that had clued me in on their plan to talk to Jed. It had only taken the suggestion of my cooperation to get them to promise to back off for now. While I had no intention of letting them talk to him, I planned to string out our talks until I got everything I wanted out of the deal. Jed's new life would never be in danger. I'd see to that.

I shot him a glare. "Maybe she wouldn't have shown up here if you hadn't told her about the Feds wanting to talk to him in the first place. I told you to keep it to yourself."

He lifted his chin, fire shining in his eyes like he was spoiling for a fight. I wasn't surprised. He'd threatened to fire me as a client a half dozen times since I'd been arrested, and I had to admit I was a shit client. I did what I wanted and ignored half of his advice. I would have fired me too.

But now he was standing his ground as he said, "I thought she had a right to know."

"You always had a soft spot for her," I said in mock disgust.

"Pot meet kettle," he shot back. He had a point. I'd always liked Neely Kate and her fiery temper. I liked the way she looked out for Rose, and I knew Jed had it for her bad, even when she was married. When he'd joined her on her road trip to Oklahoma, I'd purposely given him the ultimatum of having to choose—her or me. I knew my next phase with Hardshaw was about to kick in and I didn't want him anywhere near ground zero. I'd considered firing him, but I knew he'd never take it seriously. So, I made him choose, hoping to God he wouldn't be stupid enough to pick me over the woman of his dreams.

He didn't disappoint.

I knew I was a prick for handling it that way, but he was too loyal to leave me, even if he thought what I was doing was foolish and dangerous. He would have stuck with me to the end. This way, he got a clean break and had all the more reason to go after the woman he loved.

I have no regrets. My life doesn't have room for them.

Still, sometimes I wondered if I should regret everything that happened with Rose—from making her go to that auction to falling in love with her, but, bastard that I was, I couldn't find it in me. I loved every second of every minute I'd had with her, and I wouldn't trade all the money in the world for any of it. Even if it hurt her. Even if it hurt me.

I learned long ago that you can't change the past so there's no use dwelling on it.

And it's even stupider to wish for things you can't have.

"The reports I give you aren't enough?" he asked, and I realized I'd missed something.

"What are you talkin' about?"

"The reports on Rose and her baby. What are they lacking that Neely Kate can give?"

A personal touch. Moments about their daily lives. I couldn't be there to see my daughter grow up, but I needed more than dry reports. I needed the day-to-day details, and Neely Kate could give them to me. "I couldn't get the Feds to back off for nothin', now could I? It'll be easy enough for her to do. Plus, she'll like it."

He grumbled under his breath, then asked, "Does that mean you want me to call off the PI we have keeping tabs on her?"

"Not yet. Let's see what Neely Kate's reports actually say first."

He shook his head. "What are you up to that you're not telling me about?"

"Who says I'm up to something?"

"It's written on your face, which is sayin' something because you're usually wearing a poker face."

"So, what's my face sayin' right now?"

"That you have a plan."

I shrugged. "I always have a plan."

"That doesn't answer my question."

"Well, it's all you're gonna get for now," I said, then rested my forearms on the table. "Now tell me what you've got on Adam Kingsley."

Chapter Fourteen

Joe

I woke up on Christmas morning and found Rose's side of the bed empty. A sliver of panic shot through me before my common sense slid in and told me she'd likely gotten up with one of the kids.

The time on my phone read 6:12, so I got up and checked Hope's room across the hall. Her bed was empty, and Rose wasn't sitting in her rocking chair. I headed down the hall, poking my head in Mikey and Ashley's rooms. Both kids were asleep, and Mikey was still holding onto the stuffed reindeer Bruce Wayne had brought him the night before at our Christmas Eve dinner.

I went downstairs, purposely missing the creaky step, and found Rose sitting in an armchair with Hope in her lap. Our daughter was nestled in the crook of her arm, staring at the blinking white lights on the Christmas tree. Rose smiled at me as my feet touched the floor. When I saw her face light up in my direction, a wave of pure joy shot through my blood. I still couldn't believe she was mine. That I had three kids I was absolutely crazy about, and I was happy, so blissfully happy.

So happy but there was an undercurrent of dread always below the surface, as though I was just waiting to lose it all.

Whenever I confessed it to Rose, she'd always kiss me and tell me that was nonsense talking. That she and the kids weren't going anywhere, not unless I was going too.

"What are you doin' up?" she whispered.

I closed the distance between us and sat on the ottoman in front of her, carefully sliding her feet to the side. "I woke up and you weren't there, so I came to find you."

"You should have gotten more sleep before the kids wake up," she said in a hushed tone.

I shook my head, smiling at her. "I wanted to be with you and Hope. I don't want to miss a single moment of our first Christmas together."

She started to protest and then a frown formed. "I guess you're right. This is our first Christmas *together*."

I reached over and squeezed her hand as I picked it up. "The first of many."

Her eyes filled with love. "Many, many."

Hope's gaze shifted from the tree to me and a huge smile spread across her face. She said, "Dada" and reached her pudgy hands toward me.

Rose's eyes flew wide. "She just called you dada!"

She'd been babbling the sound, but this was the first time she'd used it in relation to me.

My heart burst as I scooped her into my arms. "I'm not sure this day could be any more perfect," I said past the lump in my throat.

"You haven't even opened your gifts yet," Rose teased with glassy eyes. "I know for a fact Mikey got you something you're gonna love." She got up and picked up her coffee cup from the side table. "I'm gonna get more coffee. Want me to bring you some?"

"Yeah," I said absently as I stood and took Hope over to the tree and pointed out ornaments to her. She tried to reach for several, but I kept them safely out of reach.

When Rose came back with two cups of coffee, I sat on the sofa and Rose sat next to me, and I wrapped an arm around her shoulders.

"How long do you think we have before the kids get up?" I asked.

"I don't know," Rose said, "but I suspect not long. While I'm enjoying the quiet before the storm, I'm eager for them to see what Santa brought them and to open their gifts from us."

I leaned my head against hers for a moment, then kissed the top of her head as I took in the pile of presents under the tree, along with the two bicycles from Santa. There was a doll house for Ashley I'd spent several late nights in the barn building, and a huge LEGO set for Mikey. Hope had a push toy to help her stand and walk.

"Thanks for being part of this," Rose said softly.

I turned to her in surprise. "What are you talkin' about?"

She shrugged, keeping her gaze on the tree. "It's just that a lot of men wouldn't be so willing to just take on fatherhood for two more kids. You never acted like it was a question."

"That's because it never was," I insisted forcefully. "I love those kids, even before they lived with us. As far as I'm concerned, they may not have my last name and they may have a father, but they're still mine and God help the person who claims otherwise."

She reached up and kissed my cheek, and I knew she knew I was thinking about my conversation with my mother. "They love you too."

"I want to do Violet proud," I said, the lump back in my throat. "She had her moments. but there was never any doubt she was a good mother."

"Agreed."

There was a clamor upstairs, the sound of little feet, and then Mikey shouted, "Get up, Ashley! It's Christmas!"

Ashley shrieked with excitement right before I heard her feet clomp across the floor.

"Ready for the chaos to start?" Rose asked with twinkling eyes.

I pressed a kiss to her lips and pulled back, basking in the love in her eyes. "I wouldn't have it any other way."

Epilogue

Neely Kate

It was the week after New Year's and Rose was out on a consult, so now seemed like the perfect time to write my letter. When I finished, I could walk it and the flash drive with multiple photos over to Carter's office. If I was feeling particularly ornery, I might not give Carter any notice and aggravate his receptionist by marching past her desk and straight to his office.

I pulled out the stack of stationary I'd purchased for just this purpose and grabbed a pen and prepared to write, only I stopped at the salutations. I couldn't make it out to Skeeter, and I wasn't writing it to Carter. I could just jump into the meat of the letter, but that didn't feel right either. "To whom it may concern" was too serious and formal, and I didn't dare write something that would call Skeeter Hope's father. He may have contributed his DNA and he might be concerned about her well-being, but Joe was her father through and through, and that was a hill I would die on.

I tapped the pen on the paper for nearly a minute, racking my brain for something until I finally settled on something that seemed perfect.

"Dear friend," I said out loud as I wrote the words. It seemed strange to call Skeeter Malcolm my friend, but there was no denying the things he'd done to help me put him in that category. Sure, he'd done some of them because I was Rose's friend, but I was sure some of them were because he liked me.

Jed still had no idea I'd gone to see Skeeter, nor that he'd been close to meeting with the FBI. Carter had warned me on the way home from the prison that I should still tell Jed and we should consult an attorney… just in case. But I trusted Skeeter. If he said Jed would be safe, he'd be safe. Maybe that was foolish, but I trusted his word. Especially since Mike had called Rose that very afternoon and told her he was giving her full custody.

Even though I hadn't told Jed about our visit, he'd immediately noticed that very afternoon that I was less stressed. He'd asked me what had put me at ease, and I'd told him I'd taken the afternoon to sort out my feelings, and that everything was fine now. While I was relieved that wasn't a lie, I still felt guilty. I hated keeping a secret from him, and this was a secret I'd need to keep for the rest of my life. Especially the once-a-month letters.

Secrets were a slippery slope. Once you let one in, it was easy to entertain another, but I swore to myself this would be the last one.

I only hoped it was true.

I turned my attention back to the paper in front of me. What would someone like Skeeter want to know? He didn't seem like a guy interested in baby development, but I wasn't going to tell him much about Rose. Telling him about Hope was one thing, but sharing intimate details about Rose seemed like a betrayal. I had no doubts that Rose would share the moments with Hope's life with him, but she wasn't going to share her own. I'd keep it to the bare basics with her. Things someone in town who was paying attention would know.

But Hope?

I decided I'd write what I'd tell a mutual friend—whether they were interested or not. Skeeter could skim parts if he wanted to.

I put the tip of my pen to the paper and began.

Dear Friend,

Hope just turned eight months old a couple of weeks ago. She's been teething like crazy, but thankfully she's not been too cranky or run a fever. She can roll over from her tummy to her back and from her back to her tummy, and while she can scoot across the floor. She's not crawling yet, but she's on her hands and knees, so it should happen any time.

She loved the Christmas lights, and she had lots of presents, but her favorite part was playing with the wrapping paper. (I've included a photo.) She's a sweet baby but can be strong willed, and literally has a hard head, as evidenced by the second photo—she head-butted Santa and broke his nose.

I got lost in the writing until I had two full pages, and realized I hadn't told him anything about Rose yet.

Rose is very grateful for what you did to get Mike to give her custody, even if she doesn't know it was you. She's obviously happier, and so are the kids. Business is booming, and she's keeping busy, but she's happy. She has everything she ever wanted and more.

I paused, then decided to throw caution to the wind and tell him how I really felt.

I know the sacrifice you made, and she does too, but I think I understand it so much more. I know these letters are the price I paid to get want I wanted, but it seems like so little. Just know that I'll be more than willing to help you in future, should you ever need my help.

I should have put more thought into that promise. I'm not so sure I would have made the offer if I'd known what he'd eventually ask of me.

Rose continues with *Trouble Comes in Threes* (Rose Gardner Investigations #8)

. . .

YOU CAN ALSO READ MORE about James adventures in *Keeper of Secrets* (Carly Moore Mystery #7). He also is a main character in the Harper Adams Mystery series, which starts with *Little Girl Vanished*.

USE the QR code to sign up for Denise's email list.

ABOUT THE AUTHOR

Denise Grover Swank was born in Kansas City, Missouri and lived in the area until she was nineteen. Then she became a nomad, living in five cities, four states and ten houses over the course of ten years before she moved back to her roots. She speaks English and smattering of Spanish and Chinese which she learned through an intensive Nick Jr. immersion period. Her hobbies include witty Facebook comments (in own her mind) and dancing in her kitchen with her children. (Quite badly if you believe her offspring.) Hidden talents include the gift of justification and the ability to drink massive amounts of caffeine and still fall asleep within two minutes. Her lack of the sense of smell allows her to perform many unspeakable tasks. She has six children and hasn't lost her sanity. Or so she leads you to believe.

denisegroverswank.com

Don't miss out on Denise's newest releases! Join her mailing list.